SKINNER

SKINNER

F. M. PARKER

W

DOUBLEDAY & COMPANY, INC.

GARDEN CITY, NEW YORK

1981

Library of Congress Cataloging in Publication Data

Parker, F. M.
    Skinner.

    (DD western)
    I. Title.
PS3566.A678S57   1981   813'.54
ISBN: 0-385-17382-2
Library of Congress Catalog Card Number 80-1863

Discard

Pawonto was a Paiute Indian who lived in the time and vicinity of the locale of this story. Pawonto, also called Willie Dorsey, was a medicine man in adult life. In point of fact, he lived to be over one hundred years old and died in the mid-1960s.

Egan was war chief of the Paiutes during the last uprising of the Indians in eastern Oregon. He was born a Cayuse, saw his parents killed in a massacre by the whites, and was raised by a Paiute family. He was killed in 1878 by the Umatillas who cut off his head and took it to the white soldiers.

General Oliver Howard, U. S. Army, was in charge of the final battle that broke the resistance of the Indians in eastern Oregon.

SKINNER

THE MAKING OF THE LAND—
A PROLOGUE

Twenty million years before man arrived on the land there was no land, only ocean. But below the salty brine the earth was alive and restless, gathering strength to shove the wet shroud aside. And finally, a bulge hundreds of miles wide swelled a section of the earth's crust. This breast of a growing continent battled and crowded the sea from its basin and exposed for the first time to the sun, massive layers of sandstone, limestone, and shale piled thousands of feet thick by the energetic waters. During the passing of a few million years, the basin that was now a large, flat plain grew a fertile cover of soil and came alive with countless species of life.

Beneath the sedimentary rock of the plain, the earth was boiling hot. Scores of ruptures tore open its hard, brittle shell, and from them gushed liquid rock, white hot and so charged with volatile gases it flowed down the slightest slope of land. It smothered square mile after square mile with a blanket of death.

The outwelling of lava, cooling from red, to brown, and finally to black, slowed to a creeping, viscous mass and stopped; and the land lay bare for century after century. The tough, hard rock did not weather enough in a thousand years to form a soil; but in ten thousand years, or even better, twenty thousand, soils did form and hardy plants invaded and took root. Hungry animals followed the invasion of the plants, drifting across the lava surface, breeding and dying, adding their small measure of change to the uncaring land.

Gigantic pressure, over thousands and thousands of years, built up again in the earth's crust. The old vents and fissures, or new ones, gaped open with unbounded force, and molten rock, unimaginably hot, flooded out. It always sought the low land, covering the previously deposited beds and flowing beyond them, trapping the panicked animals, burning them to ashes in a moment and incinerating the grasses and weeds into a thin carbon film between the rock sheets.

Each new lava flow interfingered with tongues of lava that had erupted from neighboring ruptures until the black rock smothered and hid the older sea-born rocks for an area of more than a hundred thousand square miles. After many eruptions, hard rock, thousands of feet thick, was formed, composed of one lava flow piled upon older flows.

But the earth again flexed its awesome might. It shifted, shook, and stretched the ancient sedimentary rock and the overlying lava layers. The inflexible rock crumpled and broke along deep north–south faults into massive blocks, some a hundred miles long. The force tilted the blocks, dropping their eastern edges, and at the same time lifting their western rims often three quarters of a mile or more high in vertical west-facing escarpments.

Along the sunken eastern borders of nearly all of the great blocks, rushing streams formed and cut long channels to the north. Tributary branches began at the base of the escarpments and cut deep valleys into it, sculpturing a north-to-south trending chain of rugged mountains. Rock-scouring glaciers grew on the north side of the very tallest peaks and hewed short U-shaped valleys.

One down-faulted valley was dammed by an impervious lava wall that prevented the snow and rain that fell into the basin from escaping to the ocean. The trapped water, billions of gallons, created a great lake, two hundred feet deep and seventy miles wide. The long sweep of the powerful glacial winds across the deep lake generated mighty, moving ridges of water. These lusty waves charged in upon the rock shore, and beat and ground the lava beds into a black sand and rock terrace that completely encircled the young lake.

Beneath the lake, the restless, superheated cauldron of lava had one last task to perform. It erupted up through a fissure, boiled up through the water of the lake, exploded the waves and threw columns of steam into the air. After the initial surge, the lava, cooled by the chilly water of the lake, oozed out month after month and year after year. Sometimes its outpouring slowed and at other times burst with great violence, blowing ashes into the lake and laying down ash beds upon the previously deposited lava. And then more lava, until a mountain grew a mile high in the middle of the lake.

Finally, the boiling lava fountain died away and all was quiet. The climate turned dry, and the lonely lake with its private mountain began to shrink. Each year at the end of the rainy season, it was smaller than the year before. Then the time came when no water was carried through the dry season, and all the fish died. The black lava mountain remained, surrounded by a dusty, gray-white alkali lake bottom where no plant or animal lived.

That is the way it was when man found it.

CHAPTER 1

The group of six horsemen, heavily armed with rifles and six-guns and leading an overloaded packhorse, was moving camp from Rock Corral Springs to the Honeycombs, a badlands country on the northern rim of the Alvord Desert. Their horses were tired, for they had traveled far and still had several miles to go. The men used every strip of hard ground or layer of rock they found to hide their trail, and this had lengthened their journey. But this was the last move before they pulled the job.

A strong, unpredictable late August wind thrashed the limbs of the few stunted juniper and darted around the rough, angular mounds and low hills, some a few hundred feet tall, of volcanic ash and welded tuff. It buffeted the riders, flopping their vests and shirts and causing them to cinch their hats down tightly.

The men followed the rocky bottoms of the intermittent stream channels, the only access into the rough, jagged topography. The gullies were carved and squeezed in between the more welded and enduring knobs of volcanic debris, exploded onto the landscape thousands of years before.

Of the six, only Shorty and Otley were acquainted with the high desert country of eastern Oregon. Shorty alone had the intimate, detailed knowledge required to use the mountains, breaks, and badlands and juniper thickets for cover and escape. He and a partner had rustled cows there several years before.

Otley gave the general directions of travel; but Charles French, the Canadian, led, selecting the methods and paths to ride to hide their tracks. Shorty rode third in line, followed by the Mexican, Luz Acosta; then Gillespie and last, the gun fighter, Storms. Two more men, Perrine and McClung, were riding far to the northwest returning from Bend with twelve good horses.

Anger continued to rankle in Shorty. He had agreed to a robbery; a stealthy in-force attack on a bank, followed by a fast, well-organized ride out of the country to safety on a relay of horses. Then a quick division of the loot and he would be away, free, to distant parts. Now French had changed all of that. He had ridden back the day before from the town of Westfall and told the group the new plan.

"Fellows, the bank isn't stuffed full of money like we hoped. It has only a few thousand dollars and it sure's not worth all the work and maybe getting shot for." French squatted by the fire sipping coffee, his black, button eyes shifting from one gang member's face to another.

"The silver mine is shut down at Silver City, had a cave-in of the mine shaft and no ore is being shipped. It will be two or three months before the big payrolls and ore shipment will start up again. And as you can see by the short grass on the low country, the spring and summer have been dry, so the cattlemen have decided to keep their livestock on the mountain pasture longer than usual. The fall sale of cattle won't be held until late October."

"How do you know all this?" asked Shorty, not liking what he was hearing. French didn't seem very sorry about the setback.

"It's common knowledge around town," answered French,

looking at the little man. "And I'll tell you something else I found out that isn't known by everybody; the bank moved most of its cash money, nearly a hundred thousand dollars, to the main bank in Denver. It only kept enough cash for a low level of business in Westfall. It's not going to call the money back until the cattle buyers flock into town for the fall cattle sale or the mine starts up again."

"And how did you find out about the money being moved?" asked Otley.

French grinned slyly, looking down at the Mexican clothing he had worn as a disguise while in town and had not yet changed. "One of the bank tellers got a little drunk one night. It just so happened that a friendly Mexican helped him stagger home and while being a good Samaritan, asked him a few questions which he answered."

"French, you've got something more on your mind than you're saying. What is it?" asked Shorty.

"Well, there just happens to be a rich rancher who has a granddaughter that is his only relative and she must be worth quite a bundle of money to him. Besides the ranch, he also owns part of the silver mine and I figure, from what I have found out, if we were to take the girl for a long ride out through the desert there might be as much as a seventy-five thousand-dollar ransom waiting for us when we got back."

"Where would he get the cash money since the bank has sent so much to Denver?" questioned Shorty.

"The way I figure it, the granddad could ride to Brogan and catch the train to Denver, get the money to pay the ransom, and be back to Westfall, all in four to five days."

"Is she pretty?" asked Shorty.

"Beautiful is more like it," answered French, "and looks plenty strong and able to ride fast enough to keep up without much trouble for us." He looked Shorty in the face and each tried to fathom the other's mind.

The gang talked late into the night devising the plan. Next day they moved camp.

The wild mustang band of seventeen bachelor studs nervously worked their way closer to the narrow, rocky trail that led down to the water hole. Though they had been without water for two days, they still took only a few hesitant steps at a time. For several minutes they stood, searching the wide, sagebrush-covered flat with sharp eyes, lifting their sensitive noses to gently suck in the hot air and test it for the scent of any hidden enemy. Again they moved forward a half dozen paces, following the lead of an old harem stallion that had recently joined the group after having been whipped and his mares stolen.

Skinner, watching the spooky herd of horses through a tiny opening in the top of a sagebrush, cradled the rifle in his arms and remained crouched out of sight. The burning sun beat down upon his broad back and sweat leaked slowly out from under his hat, washing muddy streaks down through the dust, thick in the stubble of his beard. He had been in this exact position for over an hour, but he waited patiently, for the horses had to have water soon and to get to it would have to pass within easy rifle shot.

The stallion's control of the males was not as complete as it had been on his band of mares. One young stud, catching the smell of the water on the wind and no longer able to deny his thirst, broke past the leader. The others immediately followed suit and, once having made up their minds to go in to drink, crowded and shoved each other to get to the water first. Their hard hooves churned up the dust and rattled the rocks on the steeply inclined trail and then splashed the water in the arroyo bottom.

Skinner let the horses drink their fill and file up away from the water toward him. As the old lead stallion came close abreast, he raised his rifle and shot him through the head. The gaunt animal fell with a thud, kicked spasmodically a few times, and then lay still. At the crack of the gun, the other horses stampeded at a dead run.

As the line of horses streamed by, he killed a lame one, then a bony pinto, and next a squat gray that looked like an overgrown pony. He shot as fast as he could make the judgment as to which one was to be killed next and lever a bullet into the firing chamber.

The horses in the rear tried to jump over the fallen and dead in front. One stumbled, then was bumped from the side and fell off the trail. He struggled to his feet and tried to escape, limping badly. Skinner shot him through the chest and he fell with a high, shrill whinny. With dogged determination he labored to his knees, held the position a moment, moaned, coughed bright red blood, and sank down dead.

Dusty wind, carrying the strong odor of manure, blood, and the fear of the horses, floated over Skinner. He stood up, and with an unfired round still in his rifle, watched the remaining animals escape.

He leaned the hot rifle against a sagebrush, pulled a small stick from his pocket, and cut five more notches in it. Marking them off methodically, he counted forty-six horses he had killed in two days. He did not like what he had done, even though he knew it was necessary for the good of the herd.

He raised his head and looked out across the broad flat and to the hills beyond. The year 1888 looked as if it was going to be a bad one. Even though it was only the last of August, the land was already bare of all vegetation except for the wilted sagebrush. The bachelors and many other horses had grubbed out every blade of grass for miles in all directions. The hungry animals traveled as many as twenty miles a day, out to feed and then back to water. He knew some, like the hardy studs, watered every second day, but the hot, dry weather drove the nursing mares and their foals to the water hole every day. Many of the younger colts, unable to travel the long distances, lay dead along the worn, dusty trails.

As a good herdsman he had to select the horses, the old, lame, and the ugly, that must die now so that those that were left would have feed during the frigid, biting winds and snows of winter. But the snow when it came, following the droughty summer when the grass had made only a small fraction of its normal growth, would be lifesaving. The wet white stuff would be used for water and the animals could abandon the few water holes that restricted their grazing areas. They could forage long distances across the valley in search of new, ungrazed grass.

Skinner worked his way through the brush to his horse, hidden in a shallow ravine a few hundred yards away. After tightening up the cinch, he mounted and guided the horse toward a round, volcanic cinder cone three or four miles away, standing like a lone, two hundred-foot-tall sentry on the level plain of the valley.

At the base of the cone Skinner stopped. He knew the horse could not climb the loose, crumbly slope so he tied it at the bottom. Lifting his canteen from the pommel and taking a telescope from the saddlebag, he struggled upward to the top.

He settled himself as comfortably as he could in the hot sun on the bare hilltop. Pulling the telescope from his pocket, he extended it full length and began to glass the sun-drenched valley and surrounding hills. The only thing that moved through the shimmering, heat-distorted view of the telescope was a small band of mares and a stallion heading for water. Though there were nine mares, there were no colts. Skinner shook his head sadly.

Slowly the yellow-white sun passed the burning zenith and shadows began to grow on the north side of the cinder cone.

A lethargic crow flapped by, turned, glided down, back-pedaled with thick black wings, and settled into the top of a sagebrush in the shade. Skinner envied him his shade, took a short pull on the hot canteen, and sweated.

He thought he saw a small puff of dust and put the scope to his eye to check it out. Under the magnification a lone rider leading five horses was plainly visible. The horses were tied in a line, nose to tail. He examined the tail of the last animal; it was uncut and extremely long, more than likely a wild horse.

"Son-of-a-bitch!" exclaimed Skinner. Someone was stealing his horses. He collapsed the telescope into his hand with a snap.

He hurried down the cone toward his horse, the reddish-brown cinders sliding from beneath his boots and rattling and clinking down the slope ahead of him. Quickly he mounted, kicked the horse down into a shallow arroyo that appeared to trend in the right direction, and followed the twisting trench, hoping to intersect the rider with the horses.

Twice he stopped and eased his horse part way up the side of the wash and peered out to determine the location of the horseman. Each time he was closer, and it appeared he had guessed correctly about the direction of the wash and if he hurried, he could head off the man without ever showing himself.

The dry stream bed suddenly made a sharp turn to the left and Skinner hesitated, trying to decide if he should proceed along the new course or check the man's position again. Then the thud of hooves of several horses drew near. He jerked his rifle from its scabbard and spurred up out of the arroyo onto the surface of the plain.

The startled rider whirled to face the noise and saw the big red-headed man almost on top of him, coming straight on.

"Hold it right where you are," ordered Skinner, his rifle

ready in his hands. "I would just like to take a look at those horses for a minute." He spoke to his mount and the animal stopped and stood rock still.

The man recovered quickly and his hard eyes watched Skinner's every move. "They are just wild horses. And anyway, what right do you have to stop a man and point a rifle at him?" He edged his horse around so he squarely faced Skinner.

"Do you know where you are and who owns all the horses in this valley?" asked Skinner.

"No, I don't know either one of those things since I came in from way over near Burns and haven't seen a man for days. And as for someone owning these horses, none have brands or marks and just by looking you can see they are mustangs. I noticed they were damn good stock so I caught a few," he motioned toward the string of high-grade animals standing in a line behind him. The man showed no fear, and when he swung his hand back from pointing at the horses, he rested it near his tied-down six-gun.

"How many horses did you see with a Lazy S on it while you were catching them?" queried Skinner. He saw the flicker of an eyelid and knew the man had seen his brand and may have actually culled the branded stock out of those he had trapped. "And did you use a rock-walled horse trap already built to capture them?"

The man remained silent, measuring Skinner. His hand had slipped an inch closer to his six-gun.

"Now, my name is Skinner and all the horses in this valley belong to me. Part of them are branded. I will let it go this time and just mark it up to ignorance on your part that you tried to take my horses, if you just turn them loose and ride out."

"Like hell I will. No man rides up like this and takes wild horses I have caught."

"I suggest you ride into Westfall and ask about this band of horses before you take it on yourself to get mean," suggested Skinner.

"I don't have to ride anywhere or talk with anybody. These horses are going with me to Burns."

"You are only going to hell if you try that."

The man swiftly plunged his hand for his gun. Skinner shot from the level of his waist without raising the rifle to his shoulder. At the close range the heavy slug slammed the man backward from the saddle. His slack and lifeless feet came free of the stirrups and he tumbled with a thump to the hard ground.

The man's horse and the five wild mustangs, all tied together, bolted away a couple hundred yards before they got tangled, two falling and pulling the others to their knees. Skinner, careful not to get kicked or bit, cut the wild ones free, and they scattered, running hard. Then he unsaddled the dead man's horse, slapped it on the rump after the other animals, and threw the saddle into a thicket of sagebrush.

He returned to the limp form of the man on the dusty ground, knelt beside him, and took his still holstered pistol and several gold coins from one of his pockets.

"I would've let you go if you had just turned the nags loose," said Skinner to the deaf ears. "Now I have the job of burying you in hundred-degree temperature without a shovel in hard ground."

It is not often a man knows when, where, and how he is going to die, reflected John Manderfield solemnly as he rode his horse slowly up the steep face of the mountain. They traveled slowly because the horse had lived through more than twenty long, cold winters and showed his age; and the man himself was very old, gaunt, and stooped. A web of wrinkles were squeezed into his pale face; and bleached blue eyes were sunk in half-hidden sockets beneath limp, gray eyebrows. The muscles of his thighs trembled slightly against the worn leather of the saddle.

The mountain was a massive block of the earth's crust, faulted and tilted. John guided the horse along its upthrown edge, the crest between the four thousand-foot, nearly vertical west flank and the gentle opposite face that sloped away for fifty or sixty miles to the east.

The route he followed dodged the squat juniper trees and giant lava boulders sprinkled on the mountainside and waded through the previous summer's growth of grass, mostly leafless stems now, all the fragile parts having been whipped away by last winter's harsh winds. Buried deep down inside the clumps of stems, the bunch grass had greened up, but had grown only a couple of inches before it died, for this was the eighth month without either snow or rain.

"God! I'm weak," John whispered to the horse. Even though he had ridden the entire distance up from his ranch house in the valley below, the elevation change made his lungs labor like worn-out bellows trying to suck in enough air to keep a red-hot forge going.

The hot wind, smelling of juniper and dead grass, fanned his face. The old horse shifted its stance; and John smiled at the familiar, solid feeling of the broad back moving between his legs. He examined the mountainside of brown grass, the dark-green juniper, the big boulders, and above all the sapphire-blue sky profiling sharp as the tooth of a saw blade the ragged mountain peak rearing high above. Never had he seen the colors so rich and their contrast so bright.

"God! It is beautiful," John spoke to the horse again and ignored his straining lungs. He shook his head as he realized that was the second time he had used the Lord's name in only a minute. Was he trying to pray?

Twisting around to look back the way he had come, he

tried to see his house in the deep valley below; but the wide bench swelling the side of the mountain blocked his view. He swung his eyes to the low desert country in the west, to the gray-white alkali plain of the Alvord Desert stretching away, mile upon mile, as far as the eye could see. In the middle of the ancient lake bottom, miniaturized by the distance, squatted one lone, black lava mountain. He had always wanted to explore that mountain, but had never gotten around to it.

The strong wind blew out of the northwest, sweeping the hotter air of the desert toward the mountain. Heated unevenly by the baking sunlight on the white earth of the bottom of the long-gone lake, the wind in places lost its smooth southeast flow and began to eddy and swirl. The swirls grew and pirouetted like invisible dancers and then, as their strength grew, birthed giant dust devils that dizzily spun white dust around and upward in vortices of counterclockwise-whirling turbulent pools of air four to five hundred feet deep. The ghostly columns, like giant dancing worms, wiggled and zigzagged along to the southeast with the wind.

"There will be a dust storm down there before the night comes," prophesied John to no one.

He reached out with a gnarled hand and clutched the saddle horn and hung on to it. The sharp pain tore through him again as it had the day before, deep in the pit of his chest where his heart, with its paper-thin walls, tortured itself in frantic contractions. He straightened his skinny body and tensed the muscles in his back, trying to pull the sag out of his slumped shoulders to give his heart more room to beat.

No use to delay any longer, he thought. Everything that could be put in order in his life had been done. Those few people he loved or owed were all taken care of in his will by the money, land, and cattle he had accumulated by hard work over many years.

He nodded his head as he made the decision. It was now time and he was ready, ready to die.

"Go, you old bastard, go," whispered John, leaning far forward until the worn brim of his hat touched the horse's gray mane. He raked his sharp, silver spurs across the bony ribs of the horse, immediately raising a long welt.

Startled and hurt, the horse sprang forward, pounding his iron-shod hooves along the narrow trail that hung precariously on the steep side of the mountain. He ran in the center of the path, carefully avoiding stepping on the loose, round rocks that would trip and throw him down the vertical side.

Satisfied for a moment, John clamped his toothless gums together, crushing his lips thin as cigarette paper, and rode with an ease born from seventy years of riding. This was the way to die, just ride the horse right off a ledge and fall into the canyon hundreds of feet below. The fall was surely long enough to kill him quickly, and no one would ever know it was deliberate. And maybe there was a happy hunting ground, as the Indians believed, where he would be reborn young and strong and have his horse and gun with him. He snickered a disbelieving laugh and shoved that nonsense from his mind.

The ribbon of path, crowded by a perpendicular ledge on the left side and a bulge of the mountain on the other flank, squeezed in between them and made a sharp right hand turn along the brink of the cliff. Horse and rider rapidly approached the hairpin turn. He pulled his hat down tightly around his gray head and began to spur again. Even though laboring and nearly falling on the steep trail, the valiant horse strained to force his weakening legs to cover ground more swiftly.

The wise old horse suddenly sensed the intent of the man. He jerked his long head to the right and then to the left, fighting the bit, and began to break stride and slow down.

But the raking, cutting spurs gouged him onward. He struggled to run on the inside of the trail, higher on the mountainside away from the ledge and the empty space dead ahead.

They fought each other along the narrow passage, the man savagely pulling the horse's rebellious head again and again to the left with one rein as he would a plow horse, trying to set him up so that when they hit the turn they would not make it. The horse strived mightily to stay to the right and continued to slow down.

The horse won, and man and beast came to a trembling halt, the sliding hooves dislodging dirt and rock that rained down over the brink of the cliff. The horse backed away a couple of steps and spread his thin, weary legs to keep from falling. His muzzle drooped until it nearly touched the ground. There was a hard rattle of rushing air in the exhausted horse's throat and his lungs heaved. Sweat ran down his sides and made a large, damp spot where it dripped and puddled in the dirt of the trail.

"You old bastard, you stubborn son-of-a-bitch. I was ready to do it. Don't you know when a body is old and worn out it should be put to rest?" John panted weakly, clutching the pommel of the saddle.

"You should be ready to die, too. For a horse, you are older than I am," he added between breaths, his sunken cheeks flushed and his thudding heart moving and shifting against his ribs.

After a few minutes, the man clutched the saddle horn and climbed wearily down. He leaned against the sweat-lathered shoulder of the horse. "Damn you," he cursed the horse in a whisper.

They rested against each other for several minutes. Slowly their strengths partially returned and their tremblings subsided. After a few more minutes, the man stood up as erect as he could and circled around and faced the horse.

"I have ridden you for over twenty years and this is the first time you ever didn't go exactly where I told you to."

Reaching out with a calloused right hand, he caressed the velvety-soft muzzle that over the years had faded from shiny black to dull gray. He stretched past the watchful eyes and rubbed the long bony jaw. The horse always had been more intelligent than most.

"Don't you know when you've had enough of life?" asked John. The horse eyed him cautiously. His mouth still hurt from the sawing steel bit and his sides from the cutting spurs.

"All right, I won't try to trick you again," and he gently smacked the animal on the side of the neck and turned and walked stiffly back along the trail. The horse plodded along behind without being told.

CHAPTER 2

Shorty was used to changes of plans and could take that. What really bothered him was the kidnapping of a woman. Any time a woman became involved in a difficult job, it always grew more dangerous and was very apt to fail. But he was broke, with less than a dollar in his pocket. He knew he had to go along.

More than a half century of years had rolled over Shorty, and thirty of those had been riding the outlaw trail. He was still alive and kicking around while much faster gunmen were dead. Little that affected his safety escaped his cautious watchfulness. Having only a few days before joined the gang, he surveyed his new cohorts carefully, measuring their weaknesses, horses, and gun skill. Already he calculated he could outdraw Gillespie and the Mexican in a fair fight.

The best horses were none too good for Shorty. Over the years he had stolen, traded, or bought, if he had to, the top-grade animal. With his small weight, at the moment less than a hundred and twenty-five pounds after the hard travel from Denver, he had always been able to escape trouble. He simply outran it.

The man called Otley, weighing over two hundred and forty pounds, rode dead in the saddle and rarely did he get off and walk, regardless of how steep the grade. Shorty knew the big man's horse was just about done in.

The welded tuff—a hard, volcanic ash partially melted together—left few tracks, and French guided the riders up the steep path beaten into it by countless hooves of bighorn sheep and wild horses. Suddenly there was a rattle of falling rocks and a curse from Otley. Shorty glanced quickly up as the spent horse in front of him staggered, crashed down on its right knee, could not catch its balance, and tumbled to the right off the narrow passage.

Otley kicked free, rolled once and caught himself on the edge of the trail. The horse, rolling and sliding, stopped with a sickening crunch, jammed up against a dead alligator juniper. A sharp stub of a limb had rammed through its stomach.

"Are you hurt, Otley?" called French.

"Only my feelings. If that horse isn't dead, he soon will be." Otley untangled himself and stood up.

He pulled his revolver, blew some dust off it, checked the hammer and trigger, flipped open the cylinder, and looked down the barrel. Then in one smooth motion snapped the cylinder into place, thrust the gun before him, and shot the dead horse through the head.

Otley half walked and half slid down the loose talus to the horse, the rocks rattling ahead of him stirring the dust and it soaring on the wind up the slope toward the other riders waiting on the trail.

"Busted my rifle stock," he angrily exclaimed, dragging the broken weapon from its scabbard, "and even bent the barrel." He heaved the useless Winchester down the hill where it fell with a metallic clatter on the rocks.

Otley uncinched the saddle and dragged it free with a powerful wrench of his broad shoulders, unsnapped the bridle, and saw his bullet had half severed one of the straps. "Damn rotten luck."

Shorty untied his red handkerchief from around his neck and mopped his forehead. Instead of putting it back around his neck, he unobtrusively spread it over the front of the saddle and up over the pommel. Everyone was watching Otley and no one saw Shorty slide his six-gun from its holster or heard the hammer click into full cock over Otley's noisiness on the rocks. The little man shoved the gun under the bandana and positioned the barrel across the front of the saddle and pointing to the left.

Otley climbed up the slope and dropped the saddle and bridle in the trail. Casually he dusted himself off, taking his time and concentrating on how to get a horse to ride.

"French, I'll ride the packhorse," suggested Otley. "I'll unload and store the supplies and ride it the rest of the way. I guess someone can come back and get the bedrolls and grub after we reach camp."

"I guess not," responded French, watching the big man carefully. To travel on into the center of the badlands, then backtrack for the supplies, and return to camp again would be thirty miles or so. None of the horses could make it today. The earliest it could be done would be late tomorrow.

"That won't work," continued French, moving his hand over the butt of his gun and letting it float there. "I'm not going to leave our supplies dumped out here until tomorrow. We might need the extra guns and bullets at any time, and the rest of the gear we need for camp tonight. It's only about ten miles or less and you can walk or ride double. And anyway, you should've got off and led your horse up that steep of a grade."

"By God, I ain't going to walk or for that matter ride double either," countered Otley. "I'm sure as hell going to get me a horse." He backed up the slope a few feet and threw a searching look down the trail at the other members of the gang.

None of the men moved. Otley glanced at Shorty, Acosta, and Gillespie, and inadvertently caught the eye of Storms. A big-toothed, hawkish grin split Storms's large mouth and his eyes became mocking and daring. Otley knew Storms could outdraw him and jerked his eyes away, wishing he had not looked at the man.

Otley examined the mounts of the other men. Gillespie's horse, somewhat shallow in the chest, had never impressed Otley as having much endurance; and Acosta, who was also a big man, had treated his animal hard and it stood with a drooping head. Shorty's big, deep-chested brute was by far the best of the lot.

Otley paced a few cautious steps back down the trail and faced Shorty. Beneath the bandana the gun barrel shifted alignment slightly. Shorty's thin face turned hard as a hatchet blade.

"Shorty, I'm taking your horse. You know the way to the hideout and can walk there by sometime not long after dark, so get down."

"No." Shorty's voice slipped out low and iced, and the sun flashed in the glasslike sheen of his eyes.

Otley spread his legs slightly. "Now, you know I'm faster than you are. So just get down and I won't have to draw on you."

"I reckon I don't want to walk," said Shorty through stiff lips.

"Listen, you little bastard, I'm going to take your horse."

Shorty smiled at the thought of his pistol, the big open end of the barrel pointing straight at the man threatening him. He was surely going to kill Otley now.

"I'll see you in hell first."

Otley drew with unsuspected swiftness. Shorty squeezed the trigger. The hurtling bullet smashed the big man high in the left shoulder, half turning him around. The exploding gunpowder of the shot ripped the handkerchief away from the gun.

Otley still continued to draw. Shorty raised his gun into the open space above the saddle for more precise aiming and shot Otley between the eyes.

As the body tumbled backward, Shorty spun his horse right and quickly swung his gun in line with French, but pointing at the ground between them. Being new with the gang, he did not know but what French might take up Otley's fight.

"Damn!" exclaimed French. If he had known Otley was going to get himself killed, he would have let him take the packhorse.

French had considered Otley as second-in-command and had planned an important special chore for him later in the game. But Shorty had surprised him, and had surprised Otley even more. Then French's cheeks creased as he forced a thin-lipped grin.

"All right, Shorty, I'm not taking up the quarrel," and he brought his hands around to the front. "I can't afford to lose you now. Only you know this country well enough to keep the posse off us."

They watched each other for a long moment.

"Let's get him buried and get on to camp," said French. He stepped down from his horse, emptied the dead man's pockets, unbuckled the gun belt, picked the gun out of the dirt, and shoved it back into the holster. Stepping across the body, he kicked the toe of his boot deeply in under the limp form and with a heave rolled it off the path. It flopped disjointedly down the steep hillside and came to rest in a cloud of dust on the gravel of the stream bottom.

"Anyone want the saddle?" he asked.

No one said a word. French waited a few seconds, then grabbed the saddle and bridle and tossed them over the hillside.

"Who wants to help bury him?"

The remaining gang members continued silent with their private thoughts.

"Hell, he won't know the difference, so there's no reason to take trouble to dig a grave." French remounted and led the way up the hill, over the ridge, and down the other side.

Manderfield walked a short distance back along the trail and stopped. When the horse came up beside him, he caught the reins and pulling on the pommel with both hands hoisted himself up into the saddle. He spoke to the animal and started down the mountain, the dusty wind flopping the wide brim of his hat and tossing the limbs of the sagebrush. Slowed down by its climb up the slope, the wind rained a fine, whitish dust onto the grass and rocks.

Two dust devils had wandered in close to the steep side of the mountain, and from his high vantage point, John could look part way down into their open funnel tops. But something more important was happening farther out on the plain; halfway between him and the island mountain a dark line of airborne dust, already half obscuring the sun, marked a swiftly advancing storm front. It was moving more rapidly at an elevation of several hundred feet than at ground level and overhung, in a dark, ominous shadow, a mile or so of still unsuspecting desert.

He saw the destruction of the dust devils was imminent and pulled his horse to a halt to watch. The ones nearer to him continued to spin and suck up dust; but closer to the front, where the storm clouds blocked the heating rays of the sun, a weak dust devil here and there would stop spinning and disappear or lose contact with the earth, exist for a moment as a free, rotating dust cloud, and then die away.

The storm line swept rapidly forward, as if a great door had been opened to free the wind and charge it with punishing the desert. It hurried onward, whipping the dry surface, overriding the spiraling dust columns, breaking and tumbling them into billowing clouds of dirt and sand which rolled and smashed like gray-white ocean breakers.

"Cows," grunted John to himself as he saw for the first time small, dark shapes, barely visible at a great distance, appear and disappear as the dust washed over them. They were traveling with the wind, off the desert and toward the mountain. Why were they on the barren land, and whose cows were they? he wondered. No cow on its own would drift more than a few hundred feet out on the alkali. These cows were at least a half mile from the grass on the foot of the mountain.

"Might as well take a look and see what is going on," he mumbled. He clucked to the horse and they made their way down the mountainside and out into the wind and dust.

Churning, grit-laden wind blinded him beyond a few feet. He held his hat on his head with his hand and felt dirt settling in his ears. A few cows ghosted past, drifting with the wind, their hair white with alkali. He had no business out in this storm and was fast losing interest in the strange cows.

A rider appeared out of the white fog not ten feet away, the nose of his horse almost touching the nose of John's. The lower part of the horseman's face was masked with a large red bandana, and a big black hat riding the tops of his ears covered all his head down to the eyebrows. Bloodshot, dust-rimmed eyes of a very young man locked on him, widening in surprise and apprehension.

John never saw the man draw, but a six-gun appeared, leveled straight at his heart. He jammed his hands high into the air and his mouth popped open. His hat went sailing away in the wind like a crippled crow. Before he could tell the stranger he meant no harm, the gun disappeared down that person's side, the large horse was reined away, and both horse and rider vanished into the pall of dust.

"Damn," exclaimed John, his heart pounding. Then he chuckled at the humor of it all. Earlier in the day he had tried to kill himself; and now when someone pulled a gun on him, he got scared and put his hands up so fast he almost tore a muscle.

He angled his horse to the southeast, out of the storm and toward his ranch in the valley below the town of Westfall. They soon broke free of the storm and began to pick their way up a broad valley strewn with large, rounded lava boulders, carried there and dumped by a stream that had at one time emptied great quantities of water into a once-existing lake.

That rider with the cattle would not be able to properly herd them, figured John. At the best, he might get them to stay somewhat together so that when they left the alkali he could find them. From the few gaunt animals John had seen, they had been without water for some time and would need a drink very soon.

He looked back down on the dry lake and the storm piling up against the wall of the mountain. Already a few cows, driven by the fierce wind up against the foot of the nearly vertical flank, were picking their way slowly around the side toward him. Making a decision, he turned his mount toward the cattle. He could at least round up the livestock and hold them until the cowboy arrived.

Soon he had the weak, thirsty animals bunched. They stood, their bodies drooping. As others emerged from the storm, they spotted their companions and, hoping they had found water, worked their way up to join them. When they discovered there was no water, they halted in fatigued resignation. John waited and watched.

Dust whipped around Peter Pipe, clogging his nose and stinging the back of his neck. On the ground the powerful wind currents tumbled and bounced clods of alkali and silt big as peas. The storm had sprung up at this, the end of the second day on the desert. Blown by the wind and blinded by the dust, he could no longer guide his cattle. He had already ridden down his father's horse and that worn-out beast now drifted before the tumult with the cows and bulls. His own horse, though younger, showed obvious signs of weariness and thirst.

Peter blinked several times to get the tears to flow and wash the alkali from his tired, burning eyes. Downwind he could see only a few feet and had given up trying to see into the wind. The oversized hat, pulled down as far as he could get it, was fastened to his head by a piece of rawhide passing through holes cut in the brim, secured to the hatband on each side and tied beneath his chin.

Water must be found today, and soon, before the night came, or he would be helpless in a strange land. The skins of the cows were already starting to wrinkle as the flesh beneath shrank by dehydration, the water sucked away by the hot wind and long miles of travel. He knew some were already lost or dead.

Peter's father had told him to cross the desert by traveling east, to enter a broad valley between two mountains and find a town called Westfall. But the wind blew him too much to the north, pushing him up against the steep face of a brooding, rocky mountain. When the dust clouds parted just right, he could see the wall of the mountain crowding the edge of the desert.

He would have liked to again pull out the map his father had drawn for him and determine how far off course he was. But the gale-force winds and dust made that impossible and he continued from memory.

The map was a very precious possession, even more precious than his pistol and horse. It was nearly two feet square and covered with symbols accurately placed as to distance and direction, and displayed an area of over forty miles in radius from Lost Mountain.

Nate Pipe, realizing he was dying and afraid for his son with his limited knowledge of the land, the land that did not forgive a mistake, spent many days drawing, measuring, and covering a whole deer hide with characters and figures. He would erase and modify as necessary. Sometimes resting for a day or more at a time, he would then recall and add some unusual but important detail such as a wet-weather spring, a natural break in a rimrock that would allow a passage where no one expected, a natural cave, a secret hidden camp with water and grass and defensible from attack, or just a game trail in steep terrain that a horse could navigate.

He gave Peter knowledge accumulated and gleaned from years of searching, always with the expectation of its use for the very safety of his life. He ransacked every nook and cranny of his memory and recorded the great storehouse of facts to help a son survive until he also knew intimately every canyon, spring, and hidden trail.

Then all the information was condensed and inscribed on a perfect piece of tanned hide. The distance scale was exact with Lost Mountain in the center. No legend existed to interpret the map; he and Peter had designed their own symbols, and thus the chart was almost useless to another man.

Peter spent many hours studying and admiring his inheritance, not just as a map, but for its symmetry, style, and form. Without knowing what art was, he knew his father had created something very beautiful. And just for him.

He shoved away thoughts of the map, but he could not dislodge his apprehension at the unknown ahead. Every time he deviated from his father's instructions, he became uneasy. Were there rustlers or renegade Indians in the mountain, like he had been told existed, waiting for him to come closer so they could steal his cattle?

The wind split the dust and a horseman, holding his hat on his head with his right hand, materialized immediately in front of him. Peter snatched his pistol from its holster. In that fraction of a second it took him to draw, he saw the surprised face of a very old man, the thrusting of both hands high into the air, and his hat flying away in the dust.

Peter caught and halted his reflex squeeze on the trigger. The squeeze, by training, he automatically began the moment he started his draw. Across the short distance he studied the wrinkled face, white head, and worried eyes. He sensed no danger there.

As quickly as he had drawn, he holstered his gun and swung his horse away. That man would never know how close he had been to getting shot. Peter trembled at the nearness of it. His dad had taught him almost too well.

The storm continued, the finer grains of dust leaking through the bandana Peter held tightly over his nose and mouth, and sucked into his lungs each time he breathed. He felt the horse stop walking and opened his sore, tired eyes a crack to see what was wrong. The sheer face of the mountain blocked his way, so close he could touch it. The lower layers of the dust-laden wind were piled up and stopped against the vertical rock, like storm waves against a reef. Higher wind currents overrode those that were stalled and, rising nearly vertically up the wall, dropped tons of the debris they had scoured from the desert but could no longer carry.

The pocket of quiet, trapped air allowed its load to settle out. That quantity, added to by the dirt raining down from the rising air above, poured earthward in sheets like a waterfall, nearly drowning Peter in dust. It piled up on his hat and then cascaded down as the brim gave way. He squinted, pulled the handkerchief tight around his nose, and kicked the horse to the right. The blinded animal bumped along the wall, ramming Peter's leg again and again into the rock.

Peter let the horse have its head. Once set in motion, it needed no further urging. It began to climb up out of the lung-clogging dust the minute it passed the end of the wall and could get a foothold. The wind started to clear rapidly once beyond the source of alkali and silt.

Peter broke free of the wind and dust just behind the bunched cattle and the old man. He rode warily toward the waiting horseman. The man put both his hands on the horn of his saddle and kept them there. Peter could see no gun.

"I thought I'd round the cattle up for you. They looked plenty thirsty and you might not know where the nearest water hole is. And the sun's got less than an hour 'til it's down." For emphasis John nodded toward the sun, a red ball on the dusty horizon, not sure how the young fellow would take his fooling with the cattle. He could still remember the pistol pointing at his chest.

Peter tried to stay alert, to watch the other man's eyes and anticipate any sudden moves. But his head felt light and woolly and he had trouble concentrating. His abused eyes did not want to focus. He gripped the pommel to steady himself.

John examined the youth sagging in the saddle. He was covered with white dust like a ghost and, like the spirit of the storm, seemed to have materialized out of nothing. He wore a large man's clothes hung on a skinny, teenage frame. The shirt cuffs were rolled up at the wrist, trouser legs turned up and tied with deer-hide thongs at the ankle, and the much too large waist cinched in with a broad belt. A tattered hat rested on the tops of his ears, and a gun belt had been cut down and new holes punched into it. The gun appeared over-size on the thin hip, but it was tied down and looked well used. Deerskin moccasins poked through the open front of the stirrups.

"Why didn't you shoot when you had your gun on me? You were all ready for it," asked John, not being able to think of anything else to say and wanting to get the young man to talk.

"My dad told me I could trust children and very old men," answered Peter. He didn't feel like talking.

"Well, I'm glad your dad told you that. You look tuckered out. Let's get your cows to some water. One of my pastures with a water hole and some old grass is about a mile over that way." John pointed across the broad, round side of the mountain.

"What will it cost me?" queried Peter, remembering his dad's caution to always ask the price.

John considered his answer carefully. If he said too high a price, the young man might think he was trying to cheat him, and if too low, it was a trick. "Ten dollars for five days. By that time, your cows will be rested and you can move them on," he answered.

"That seems fair enough," Peter said in response to the old man's offer. "Have you seen a gray gelding come out of the storm?"

"No, nothing but these cows."

"What's up that way, up to the north along the mountain?"

"No water there." John shook his head. "If you had a horse go that direction, he's got trouble. This storm will die down tonight, and we can look for him tomorrow."

"That was my dad's horse," said Peter.

John could barely hear the low, sad words of the boy.

"Did you count the cattle? How many are there?" asked Peter.

"Forty-three."

"I lost five then."

"Too bad. Shall we go?"

The boy nodded, and they rode up behind the cattle and herded the weary animals along through the sagebrush.

They shoved the cattle through the wire gate and into a pasture straddling the creek. After they were sure all the animals had found the spring in the rocky bottom of the stream, they headed toward the large, stone ranch house, visible in the edge of the juniper on the bench above.

As they approached the long, rambling house, a fat Mexican pushed through a wooden gate in the whitewashed fence surrounding the house and walked toward them. Peter wobbled in the saddle, his eyes refusing to focus and head dragging him down as if it weighed a ton. John saw the boy about to fall and motioned with a swift jerk of his hand for the Mexican to hurry to them.

Miguel moved fast, caught Peter, and easily lifted him in his big arms.

"Don't weigh as much as a sack of beans," he observed.

"Yes, he looks like he has been on short rations for some time. But he will fill out and be a fair-sized man one of these days. Carry him to the bedroom at the end of the house," directed John.

Miguel carried the limp form through the doorway and laid him on a blanket-covered bunk.

John stood looking down on Peter. "We've got to get some water into him." He dipped a tin cup of water from a bucket on a table near the bed and, while Miguel propped the half-unconscious Peter up, put the cup to his parched lips.

"Drink!" ordered John, forcing the mouth open. Carefully, so as not to strangle the youth, they gradually got the whole cupful down his dry throat, and then a second one.

"Let's strip him down and cover him with a blanket so he can sleep," said John.

"Damn! Look at those scars!" exclaimed John, holding the half-removed pants and pointing to a mangled area big as his hand on the naked left thigh. "Not very old either," he added, indicating the fresh, purplish-red color of the flesh.

"Look here, too," whispered Miguel, holding open the un-buttoned shirt and exposing four long parallel scars extending from the top of the left shoulder down to the bottom of the rib cage. The small, brown nipple protruded at an unnatural angle from the top of one of the ridges of the scar.

"Looks like he got mixed up with a mountain lion," said John. "Let's cover him up now and let him rest."

CHAPTER 3

Peter awoke slowly, floating up out of his sleep of exhaustion. It was a pleasant, effortless rise up through the levels of his slumber. He almost surfaced to full consciousness, but felt so warm and comfortable that he relaxed and began to drift back under. But his mind, once nearly awakened, refused to go all the way down and hovered there halfway between sleep and wakefulness.

Somewhere nearby a bee buzzed and buzzed. The drone did not vary, and idly he wondered why the bee did not fly away. The buzzing recalled memories of the pink cliff roses on the mountain above the cabin where he and his father had lived. Where the honeybees, dipping into the centers of the flowers, sucked up the sweet nectar and attached the grains of yellow pollen to the hairs of their rear legs until they looked as if they were carrying round nuggets of gold. They became so heavily laden with their treasure they could hardly fly. His father had told him that was why, once they were loaded, they flew such direct routes back to their hives; the bee could not afford to waste strength by deviating from a straight line.

A small bud of worry grew in Peter's mind. Where was he and was he safe? From the feel of the bedcover, he knew he was naked. How did he get into bed? The worry blossomed and it had a tinge of alarm. Not uttering a sound, he opened his eyes.

He listened intently. Nothing but the bee stirred. The only thing he could see was the roof directly overhead and, following along the ridge beam with his eyes, a stone wall made from slabs of black lava.

He mentally checked his physical condition to see if he was fit for action. His mouth was dry, and he was very thirsty. His eyes were sore. But otherwise he felt strong. With one quick movement, he sat up and swept a searching look around the room.

A window was shrouded with a blanket, the only door closed, and the room full of shadows. He sat on a narrow wooden bunk. To the right, a few feet away, was a low table crowded with his washed and neatly folded clothes, his hat, gun and gun belt, and a wooden bucket with a long-handled dipper sticking out of it. There were three chairs and an old oak wardrobe in the room, all shoved back against the wall as if to give whoever normally lived there plenty of space to move about. The bee continued to buzz, trapped between the blanket and the window.

Peter swung his feet onto a cool, earthen floor and walked to the table. Unfolding his big trousers he stepped into them and was nearly lost in their largeness. He slid the belt through the loops, and as he buckled the belt he noticed he was another hole smaller around the waist than he had been when he started on the cattle drive. One of the first things he had to do was get some clothes that fit.

He lifted up the stack of $20 gold pieces, counted and found all seven were there, and thanked the honest person who had cleaned his clothes. Well, old man, Peter thought, you are probably the one responsible for all this and I am in your debt. He drank nearly a quart of cool water from the long-handled dipper.

Someone had brushed the dust from his hat and cleaned his pistol, leaving a thin covering of protective oil. He released the catch on the side of the gun, swung the cylinder open, and slid a bullet into each of the six round holes. The holster was dusty down inside and he took the tail of the freshly laundered shirt and began to wipe it clean.

John silently opened the door as he had done half a dozen times during the past twenty-four hours. The young man, smaller than average size, stood near the table cleaning his holster. His well-developed, ropelike muscles rippled across the naked arms and shoulders of the thin body, but a body that appeared to be in superb condition.

Peter sensed the stir of air in the room as the door opened. He turned toward it swiftly, his reaching hand almost to the gun before he recognized the voice.

"Well, well, finally awake," said John and, without waiting for an answer and ignoring the grab for a weapon, he continued talking. "If you want to take a bath, there has been a tub of water warming in the sun all day, just waiting for you. It's just outside the door and around the house to the left." He pointed to the wall on the end of the room as if Peter could see through the wall, if he knew just where to look.

"Thank you very much, sir, for all the help you have given me," said Peter, remembering his father's instructions to always thank those who were kind. He also remembered the advice to try and find out if the person being helpful had hidden reasons that would do him harm. So far, he could detect none. Then he had an afterthought: this would be true if his cattle were still safe.

"I surely need a bath. A long soak and then a bath is probably nearer the truth, to get all the dirt off," Peter grinned back at the blue-eyed old man smiling friendly-like at him and showing a flashing white set of false teeth as he stood in the open doorway. Beneath the smile the man's wrinkled face seemed strained.

Peter picked up his shirt, moccasins, and gun belt and followed the slump-shouldered figure around the house to a large, wooden tub, nearly full of water, resting beside a flat, smooth rock four or five feet in diameter. He dropped his gear on the stone.

"Come down to the kitchen on the other end of the house when you're finished, and we will have something to eat and talk awhile," said John as he turned and walked away.

"I'll be there right away, sir," called Peter, his hunger rising sharply at the mention of food. He slipped out of his pants, stepped into the tub, and sat down. The lukewarm water rose to his waist and he sighed with the pleasurable feel of water on his skin.

He bathed his sore eyes gently. Then with a piece of toweling he wet himself all over. He stood up, scooped a handful of soft soap from a bowl, and began to lather himself.

His skin prickled across the back of his neck, and he knew he was not alone. Something or someone was behind him. Quickly he whirled around.

A beautiful human, a female, stood near the corner of the house openly staring at him. Peter felt his anger begin to rise at someone slipping up on him and not making his, correction, her presence known. But the anger died almost before it could form. The young woman, about his age or slightly older, was ten times more beautiful than any animal he could remember ever seeing. His breathing slowed and he remained very still, as if she were a deer he had come upon and did not want to spook into flight.

From her head to her feet he swept his eyes, drinking in the sight of copper-yellow hair, lightly tanned, flawless skin, large blue eyes so perfectly round they appeared strange—eyes the same shade of blue as the old man's, but, God, how much prettier in this face than in that other, seamed and wrinkled, one.

Her full mouth broke into a smile, showing perfect white teeth. A puff of wind billowed her light yellow dress, and she pressed it against her thighs to control it. Then as the wind died, she put her hands on her hips.

Time slipped quietly by. The soapsuds dried and shrank in the parched desert breeze, pulling and tightening Peter's skin, reminding him he was naked. But he would not be the one to break the spell.

"Beautiful, beautiful," the words involuntarily escaped out of him. His father had not told him just how appealing women really were.

She smiled more broadly. "So you are the stranger my grandfather has been talking about?" He stood before her, again unconscious of his nudity, and his naturalness and lack of inhibition caused her to ignore it also. In any other situation she would have been terribly upset and self-conscious about walking up on a naked man.

Peter nodded. "Yes. He has been very kind to me. He helped me when I really needed it, and I am greatly in his debt."

He has an odd way of talking, she thought, each word deliberately and distinctly spoken as if he were placing something fragile upon a hard surface. Someone had taught him very well. She inspected the scars marring his leg and shoulder and noted each rib could be counted on the thin body. But no longer could she stand talking to a naked man; even if he was not self-conscious, she was.

"I'll see you at supper." She gave a small wave of her hand and disappeared around the corner.

Peter sank back down into the tub and sat looking at the place where she had vanished. He wished she had not left so soon. Then after a few minutes he finished bathing and dressed in his father's oversize clothing, rolling up the shirt sleeves and cuffs of the pants. He pulled his long brown hair, still damp, back behind his head and tied it with a strip of rawhide. After strapping on his pistol and tying the holster down to his leg, he walked along the front of the big stone house with its carved, freshly painted wood trim, looking for the kitchen. A rich man's house, thought Peter.

From the sun's height in the western sky, he calculated it was nearly five o'clock. The mouth of the valley lay to the northwest and he looked down its length. To his pleasant surprise he saw his mountain, just a black spot far out on the alkali desert. The mountain reminded him of his father.

"I am in a new life, Father, with just a few remembered instructions from you to guide me and help me survive among other people," he thought.

"Come in," said the man's voice through an open door, interrupting his thoughts of his past home.

Peter stepped inside a large kitchen. A small Mexican woman stirred something in a pan on a large stove. The man and girl came around a long table loaded with food to greet him.

"I really haven't had a chance to introduce myself. I'm John Manderfield," and he stuck out his hand and shook the one Peter extended to him.

"And this is my granddaughter, Beth Manderfield. She lives here with me."

Peter again shoved out his hand and took the small, soft hand quickly offered to meet his own. He stood and held it, looking into the girl's eyes, so large and blue they were that he felt he was tumbling forward into them. For a moment he could not speak, and his body seemed to be frozen into position. A faint smell of roses wafted from her. Did all women smell of roses? He sifted through his memories of the few times he had encountered women, a long time ago before he had gone to the mountain with his father, but could recall no odor, pleasant or otherwise.

"What is your name?" asked Manderfield, when Peter did not volunteer it. A trace of a smile flitted across his face at Peter's reaction to Beth.

"Peter," he said, looking from Beth to the old man, and then for a second he could not remember the rest of it; it had been so long since he had used it. "Peter Pipe," he finished.

Manderfield's eyes blinked twice rapidly at the name. Then he smiled again.

"Well, Peter Pipe, set down and Yolanda will serve you the best food in this part of the country."

Peter could only grin at the friendly smile and easy engaging manner of Manderfield. Yet he could not help but feel the old man seemed surprised at his name.

Peter ate the delicious food with high relish. At last, with a belly full, he laid down his fork and looked at John and Beth who were both openly watching him.

"Just as good as you said it was, Mr. Manderfield. I must find a way to repay you. Maybe it isn't polite to ask, but why are you so generous to me?"

John did not answer. How could he tell Beth and Peter he needed some change in his life, some adventure for a sick, old man, so he would not kill himself? "You looked like you could use a friend," he said, guiding the subject back to Peter. "Where did you come from with that bunch of cattle?"

"How long did I sleep?"

"A full day, twenty-four hours, straight through."

"Then that makes three days ago I started out from Lost Mountain—I guess that is what you also call the mountain out in the middle of the big desert—with forty-eight cows and bulls. I planned to drive them to a town called Westfall and sell them. I believe that town is somewhere near here—is that true?"

"Yes, it's up the valley a couple of miles where the valley bottom widens out, and the mountain is called Lost Mountain and the desert Alvord. I noticed none of the cows were branded. Don't you have a brand?"

"My dad was going to help me brand them, but he never did get well enough to stand the work of helping me rope and throw them. So we just let it go. There was just the two of us, and anyway, he said we could sell them even if they didn't have a brand. The few cows we took with us when we went to the mountain years ago had marks. Dad told me to leave them and the young calves on the mountain when I left, and that way there would be more cattle when, or if, I ever go back. And anyway, they were too old for the trip."

"Where is your dad now?" asked Beth.

"Dead," answered Peter. "He died two years ago and I buried him on the mountain." Quickly he blinked his eyes to keep the tears from forming. He was surprised that the memory still hurt so much. "I didn't even have a casket and had to bury him just wrapped in a blanket."

"I'm sorry," said Beth slowly, picturing the boy digging the lonely grave, lifting his father's wrapped body, and laying it in the bottom and then shoveling rock and dirt in upon the blanketed corpse.

"Then you have lived the last two years by yourself?" she asked.

"Yes, by myself. And before that my dad and I had been on the mountain and run cattle for about three years, ever since I was twelve years old. We went out there with eight or ten cows, and a couple of bulls, all that we had left after Dad was shot and robbed. Dad never was well after he got shot." He shifted his thin hands on the tabletop and looked at the rolled-up cuffs of his dad's oversize shirt.

"I know I look odd in my dad's clothes, but I outgrew my own and I started wearing his." He fell silent. For a period of two years there had been nobody to talk with and now he was afraid he was talking too much.

"What did you think and do in that long time by yourself?" asked Beth, her own eyes moist.

"Looked after the cattle, cut as much grass for hay as I could by hand for the winters, and hunted. You may not believe it, but there are quite a few deer on the mountain and a few mountain lions."

"Is that where you got the scars?" queried John.

"Let me tell you about that," said Peter, feeling himself relaxing with the kind and interested people. "Dad liked pistols better than rifles and we had a lot of ammunition for his handgun. But not so many shells for the rifle, and I ran out shortly after he died. Then the trouble started. Usually the lions killed deer for food, but one started killing calves. Killed and ate three before I got onto his tracks one day and followed him in a light snow. I only had bullets for this pistol, and I knew I had to get him real close or I never could kill him. All that day I trailed him. Finally he went into a big jumble of rocks, some half as big as this house, where they had broken off a cliff face and fallen down. I went in after him. When I came around this one big boulder, he jumped on me. I didn't know it at the time but I had him trapped in a dead end, and the only way for him to get out was over me. Well, I shot him once while he was sailing through the air. Then he landed on me, knocked me down hard, and sank one set of claws in my leg and another in my shoulder. He made a grab for my face, but I ducked and he got a mouthful of Dad's big, old hat. Take a look at the holes in it the next time you see it. But that mistake of his gave me time to empty my gun into him, and he dropped dead right on top of me. I had to roll him off."

Beth caught her breath and looked wide-eyed at him. John could picture this small young man firing his pistol again and again into the lion.

"You seem to be able to handle that pistol very well," observed John, recalling the speed and deftness of the draw of the gun in the dust storm the day before.

"My dad was really good. He taught me every day for three years, right up until he died; and I went right on practicing after that by myself. Dad said I had a natural instinct for it."

"Did the lion hurt you?" asked Beth. "The scars look bad."

Peter laughed, recalling that she knew about the scars because she had seen him without his clothes on. "I passed out for a few hours. When I did come to, it was dark, and it being dark and me hurt, it took me a long time to get back to my horse, which I had tied down below the rocks. Finally I got to him, climbed on, and he carried me back to the cabin. I must have been out of my head for several days. When I came around I was about dead from thirst and hunger. Infection had set into the wounds and they were full of pus. I managed to mix a poultice. After using that on the wounds for three days or so, I finally killed the infection. I just wished there had been someone around to pull the flesh back in place and sew me up. I was unconscious so long the flesh was already healing and big scars were forming when I came to."

"Well, what next, Peter, now that you have got your cattle across the alkali?" questioned John.

"I'm going to sell them and buy me a ranch," Peter said proudly. "How much will that cost?"

"A cattle spread that a man could run, with one hired hand helping part time during branding and haying, would cost about eight to ten thousand dollars. There is still public land you can graze free, without any cost, if you get away from town a few miles."

"How much will these cows bring?"

"Twenty-eight to thirty dollars each. There is one buyer in town, named Morcom. You can usually find him at the stock-yards or hotel."

"Would you do me one more favor? When I go to sell the cows in a couple of days, would you go with me?"

"Be glad to. And you can stay here until then."

Beth smiled and nodded approval.

Peter smiled back. "Well, I thank you for that. I need a lit-tle walk and think I will go down and look at the cattle. Did you see anything of my other horse?"

"Not yet, but I have Miguel out riding to the north trying to find it."

Peter nodded and got up from the table and walked out-side. Beth watched him go and then turned to the man.

"Grandfather, you acted as if you knew the name Pipe. Do you know who Peter is?"

"I think so. There was a gunman, a bank robber, rustler, just a general all-around bad guy around here a few years back. He disappeared after being shot rustling cattle."

"Oh no!" exclaimed Beth. "Whose cattle were they?"

"Mine."

"Did you shoot Peter's father?"

"Yes. That was back when I ran more cattle than I do now. Rustlers were stealing a lot of cows and the sheriff and I were out riding. Over there near Freezeout Ridge, we ran across this fellow driving a small bunch of my animals. When he spotted us, he took off fast and we started blazing away with our thirty-thirties. He slumped down like he was hit or just trying to make himself a smaller target, I didn't know which. It was late in the evening and getting dark and we couldn't trail him. We went back the next day for another try, but he was too smart for us and we could follow his tracks for only a short ways. Never did find out if he was shot, or if so, how bad. From the way he trained Peter to handle a pistol, I am glad I was not close enough to use a handgun, though he seemed more anxious to get away than to fight. He was never known to shoot anyone."

"Oh, Grandfather, what would Peter do if he found out?"

"I don't know, and don't you blame him for what his father did."

"Will you help him, Grandfather? He has been away from people so long that anybody can take advantage of him."

"Sure, you can bank on me helping where I can, girl, but from what I have seen of young Mr. Pipe, he'll do all right and not many people will get the better of him in a deal."

CHAPTER 4

The sun was already well past the zenith and sinking toward its nighttime bed in the pit below the horizon when Peter left the house and walked toward the corrals. All day the sun had shone down from a cloudless sky, and the wind chasing across the mountainside was hot. Out over the edge of the desert, a long-necked buzzard, riding a hot updraft of air, with broad wings extended and fixed, soared round and round, its darting, telescopic eyes searching for carrion on the ground a thousand feet below.

Peter tossed the saddle upon the broad back of his roan horse and cinched it up vigorously. He felt rested and relaxed after eating, sleeping, and just lazing around for two days. His long conversations with Beth and John had been enjoyable and informative; especially the evening ones which slanted away more and more from cattle, weather, and people to places far away, wars in other countries and touching on religion as the night deepened and the hours grew late. They were educating him to the current world in a most pleasant way. But he felt like a change this evening, and now was a good time to ride into town to buy new clothes and get his long hair shortened.

Miguel had not found his second horse. The fat man had returned from two days of searching, saddlesore and hungry.

He assured Peter he had checked every water hole the horse could have used. Peter believed the man had made a valiant effort and thanked him heartily, but he missed the horse. Old and familiar things, one after another, were vanishing from his life; soon he would be completely alone in an unfamiliar new world.

He swung lightly up into the saddle and sat gazing out across the sun-drenched desert toward Lost Mountain. Had it only been five days since he had left? He remembered clearly the exact moment when he had made the decision to strike out from the loneliness of the mountain and seek out a new life.

The gentle wind of Lost Mountain had been blowing directly in his face as he had hunted quietly along through a hillside of large juniper trees mixed with sagebrush. Rounding a large juniper, he startled a doe and twin fawns browsing on a dark green clump of bitterbrush. They jerked to attention with ears thrust forward, not thirty feet in front of him. Sagebrush hid their legs; the one large and two small gray bodies floated on top of the brush, silent and tense.

Peter's practice and training with the pistol had been going on for several years under the critical eye of his father. During the last year of the man's life, as his health failed, Peter consistently outdrew and outshot him. After his father's death, Peter continued to drill nearly every day, running through the various stances and positions, in daylight and dusk, striving hard to improve as if the critical and demanding eyes were still upon him. His thumb always carried a callus from cocking the hammer, and the pistol was as much a part of his hand as his finger.

One lesson had been taught over and over—how to pick out of a group of men which one was the leader and would give the signal to his cohorts to begin the fight, if it were to come to that. Now Peter watched the doe as if she were the leader of three men. He decided the first wiggle of one of her ears would be the sign that the draw and the duel would start.

The doe's right ear flicked. Peter drew and fired at her in one smooth flash. Shifted, fired again, catching the nearest fawn in the front of the chest before it could bound away. Spun farther around, fired again, and the second fawn folded at the peak of its first jump, crashed down into a sagebrush, twisting its elegant neck back along its side with a sickening crack. The stricken doe stirred. He whirled and shot her through the head, the bullet crashing through the skull.

He quickly released the cylinder of the pistol, ejected the empties, and shoved in four fresh shells. Hurry, just like his father had told him; always be ready. Smoke of burned powder still hung about him in a pall and he was already reloaded.

None of the animals moved. He examined all and found his shots had gone true to his intended points of aim. He had that feeling of assurance of his skill that only competent men really ever know, but he was surprised at the doe requiring two shots. Would a man have been able to shoot him while he had been finishing off the last two?

Peter watched the blood ooze from the hole in the doe's head. The dead young fawns looked so small and defenseless. Suddenly a great sadness engulfed him. Why had he killed? For less than a second of practice, three beautiful, living creatures were now just so much meat. Tears welled up and cascaded down his cheeks.

Sobbing shook and wrenched his body as sorrow for the deer, his dead father, and his own terrible loneliness overwhelmed him. He stood looking out beyond the desert where other men lived and cried for several minutes, his throat aching and face wet.

I will leave the mountain tomorrow, he vowed, and search out other men and be with my own kind.

Peter reined the horse away from the direction of the desert and his memories and kicked him into a comfortable rocking lope up the valley along the rutted wagon road. The big horse, well rested and fed, covered the two miles to Westfall in a few minutes.

The town straddled the well-used road which continued on up the valley, climbed across a low saddle east of the settlement, and disappeared. Consisting of several wooden buildings, some rather big, the town was much larger than Peter had expected.

Near the center of the cluster of structures, where the business of the town concentrated, a sidewalk of heavy wooden planking flanked the dusty road on both sides for a hundred yards or so. A new section of walk was being added farther down the street where fresh-sawn, flesh-colored lumber marked a two-story building under construction. A dozen or more private dwellings lined a second street on a bench above town. From their sizes, rock foundations, and gingerbread trim, they apparently belonged to the most prosperous residents. Two new residences of pretentious size were being framed up.

Peter tied his horse to the first hitching rail he came to. Not having been in a town for five years, he decided to walk its full length, refreshing his memory of what a town was really like. A small, black dog scurried out from under a porch of one of the houses and stuck his nose between the pickets of the yard fence and silently watched him pass.

Peter stopped in the shade of a tall cottonwood tree and examined the rutted dirt street, dry and dusty in the long drought. Several horses tied to hitching rails along the sidewalks, occasionally flicking flies with their tails, stood patiently waiting. A wagon with high sideboards was being loaded by a sweating man in front of one of the larger buildings. Five or six men lounging in the shade of the building watched him finish and drive away.

Another man, a little farther down the street, sat on the sidewalk and leaned back against the building, his long legs stretching out across the planking. He was eating something from a glass jar, the sunlight reflecting from the shiny surface now and then in sharp, silver rays. Two women, lifting their dress tails up out of the dust, crossed the street.

Peter's recollections of towns were pleasant, but he was tense at being near so many strange people. He drifted slowly up the street, his dad's big denim pants drooping like a faded blue bag below the belt and his oversize shirt puffing in and out in the afternoon breeze. The large hat came down to his eyebrows, and the wide brim shaded the entire length of his face. He saw the well-fitting clothes of the men as he passed and made up his mind to return quickly after his exploration and buy all new gear.

"Well, well, what have we here," called a man's derisive voice behind Peter. "What is that inside a man's clothes? Is it someone trying to act like a full-grown man or trying to hide in a man's duds?"

Peter was not sure the man was talking to him. But the reference to clothes caused him to stop and turn around inquiringly. A tall man with a smirk on his long face stepped down off the sidewalk and strode out into the street. Two others separated from the loungers grouped in the shade and joined the first. They both grinned broadly, showing yellow, tobacco-stained teeth.

"Look at that big pistol," taunted the first. "Ain't you afraid it will pull you over in the dust and get those pretty duds all dirty?"

The intent of the men was not fully clear to Peter, but a

strange, hot flush stole across his face. He measured all three. The second two had the same build and face as the first and he wondered if they were related. His father had told him blood relatives were more likely to stick together in a fight. He surveyed the other men, now silent and motionless on the sidewalk. A couple were grinning in expectation.

"Say, I believe there ain't anybody in those clothes. It's just a pair of pants, a shirt, and a hat floating down the street. Let's take them off to be sure," mocked the first, glancing quickly to his side and laughing to the other two beside him.

"Never get angry, never get angry," the long-ago instructions slipped through Peter's mind. But no one was going to take his pants off. A cold tickle ran up his spine, and the rims of his nostrils turned frosty white.

He turned squarely toward the men. All wore pistols in their belts. But they did not seem really ready to draw as he had seen his father stand when they practiced against each other. He could not interpret the difference between the threatening words and the unprepared stance of the men to back them up.

Then the talkative one tensed and his hand moved closer to his gun. "You wouldn't be considering going for a gun now, would you?"

Peter fully understood that hostile move. He shifted slightly left to face that man. If the man's hand moved one fraction of an inch closer to his gun, Peter would shoot him. Without taking his eyes off the man, he mentally measured the distance he would have to swing to bring his gun in line with the other two.

Was it going to be like on the mountain? Would he cry as much for the dead men as he had for the three deer?

The man sitting on the sidewalk stopped eating and watched the actions of the men in the street. He observed the young fellow's lack of comprehension of what was happening when the first insults were thrown at him and his uncertainty of how to respond. But then the interpretation and decision for action showed plainly, and so did the subtle shift to readiness for gun play. No fear showed on the youthful face, only a studied, deadly seriousness, a sure and certain purpose. He was going to shoot the three, or at least try to.

"Don't draw," said a voice behind Peter and off to the side. "They're just fooling with you."

Peter did not relax; it might all be a trap. He stayed locked into the man's eyes, watching for any sign he might give to signal the others he was starting his play.

"They're only kidding around. Don't shoot them," said the voice.

"Stay out of this, Skinner," ordered the first man. "If this kid wants to draw on us, that's his bad luck."

At this close range Peter knew he could shoot the man's eye out if he wanted to. With a quick, nearly invisible movement, he drew and fired. The roar of the shot reverberated between the vertical faces of the buildings. The men jerked to startled attention. The bullet smashed the still-holstered gun of the man directly in front of him and drove it backward and upward along the sloping, outward curving leather at the rear of the holster. The pistol flipped end over end into the dust of the street. The instant he triggered the first shot, Peter swung the barrel to the center of the next man. That individual had not yet begun his draw. He swung farther, onto the third. That person's hand was still six inches from the butt of his gun, and he froze it there in shocked surprise when he looked down the barrel of Peter's six-gun.

Peter did not understand how he could have beaten all three so easily. His father, even when very sick, would have had his gun out by the end of the first shot. He rotated quickly back toward the first man, but watched all of them.

All the color had drained from that one's frightened face. His hands and lower jaw trembled as if he was freezing.

Peter shifted the gun slightly and it roared again. The man's hat jerked away from his head and sailed into the dirt, erupting a puff of dust. He blanched even whiter and stood still as frozen water.

"I could have shot all of you," Peter's voice came out in a harsh, jerky whisper. "You dumb bastards, you almost made me kill you." His furious voice nearly broke and he stood threatening them with savage eyes.

"Go away. All of you get away from me," he ordered.

Unbelieving as to what had happened and the speed with which it had occurred, they hesitated for a moment, then twisted away and trotted hurriedly down the street.

"Leave it alone," Peter shouted as the first man slowed a fraction of his speed to pick up his gun and hat.

Quickly he reloaded and slid the pistol loosely into his holster. The men on the sidewalk shuffled their feet self-consciously when he swept a hard eye over them. None seemed interested in contesting him.

He turned to where the voice of the man called Skinner had come from. A big, rawboned man with red hair sat on the sidewalk holding a quart jar of canned peaches. He was dusty and several days' growth of bristly, red beard hid his face. With a long-bladed hunting knife he speared a yellow peach half and shoved the whole piece into his mouth. He chewed deliberately and met Peter's stare with amused cat-green eyes.

Skinner stopped chewing and swallowed, the sweet, slick fruit sliding easily down his throat. "There's nothing better than peaches in syrup after a long trip on the desert. Want one?" and he held out the jar of fruit.

Peter hesitated for a couple of seconds, then strode across the planking and squatted down beside him. He flipped open his big jackknife and from the offered jar fished out a peach and ate the savory delicacy.

"Good and sweet," said Peter. They ate in silence, passing the jar back and forth between them until it was empty.

"I'm glad you spoke up and said what you did," said Peter. "I would have hurt them. What were their names?"

"Fettus," answered Skinner. "They're a little mean, not too bright, and slow with a gun; but you watch out for them, for they'll try to get even with you."

"Are they brothers? They look a lot alike."

"Yep, and always ganged up in the same dirty trick."

"I'm glad they didn't try to draw against me, but why did they just stand there and not try?"

Skinner guffawed deep down. "Maybe they didn't have time," and he looked at Peter with a twinkle in his eye. "That was a tricky shot, blowing that hat off his head. Suppose you had misjudged where his head was?"

"Aw, there was at least two inches of hat above his dumb skull—plenty of room to put a bullet through without hitting anything else." Peter sensed an interest and friendliness in the big man.

"Well, well, here comes Sheriff Gumert," observed Skinner. "Looks worried."

Peter looked in the same direction. A short, powerfully built man wearing a very broad-brimmed hat strode purposefully across the street. At each step, puffs of dust geysered up around his boots and splashed his pant legs.

Sheriff Gumert stepped up on the sidewalk, planted his feet firmly, and stared down at the two seated men. "Skinner, did you do that shooting?" he asked in an unnecessarily loud voice.

Skinner looked up at him and let the seconds drag by, then spoke in a condescending voice. "No, Sheriff, this young fellow here was being aggravated by the Fettuses and he had to back them off a little bit. Didn't take much, once they figured they might get hurt. Can you imagine, Sheriff, they threatened to take his pants off right in the street." And he laughed.

The sheriff saw nothing funny in the situation and turned his full attention to Peter. Every child and adult in town, and, for that matter, for several miles in all directions, was known by him. This fellow did not belong.

"Who are you and what are you doing in Westfall?" he questioned.

Peter remembered his father's instructions that he should be polite to sheriffs, but always be cautious around them. "Sir, my name is Peter Pipe and today I'm in town to buy some new clothes. Tomorrow I will be back to sell my cattle." Again, as when he told Manderfield his name, he saw that recognition of his name flash across the sheriff's face.

"What is your dad's name?"

"Nate."

"Where is he now?"

"Sir, he is dead. Both of my parents are dead. My mother died several years ago and my dad just two years ago."

"How do you know he is dead?"

Peter was surprised at the question, and it showed on his face. "I buried him myself, that's how I know."

The sheriff studied Peter's anxious young face for a long time. "It's dangerous to other people to shoot a gun in town. How old are you anyway?"

"Sir, there were three of them and all bigger than me," answered Peter wanting to fully explain why he had drawn his gun. "And, I'm seventeen."

"I haven't seen any strange cows around. Where are these cows you want to sell?"

"They are in a pasture over at Mr. Manderfield's."

"You know John Manderfield, eh?" Peter sensed a lessening of hostility in the rough voice.

"Yes, sir, I'm staying with him."

Sheriff Gumert did not know how to interpret the boy's presence at Manderfield's ranch in light of the way the boy's father had been shot that day years ago. But he intended to find out. "Well, keep that gun in your holster or I'll take it away from you if you use it again in this town."

Both Gumert and Skinner saw the sudden stiffening of the boy's muscles at the sheriff's threat. No one, not even a lawman, was to be allowed to take his gun. Peter stood up slowly and, with rock-hard eyes that had lost all desire to be agreeable, stared the muscular lawman full in the face.

Skinner recognized the wild, unpredictability of the strange young man. He spoke in a calming voice. "Now, Sheriff, Peter here only did what anybody with any backbone would have done." Then his voice turned flinty hard. "You would be headed in a better direction if you ran those Fettuses out of town or threw them in jail for a few days for all their meanness. If they bother my friend here anymore, I may be forced to take a hand myself to show them the errors of their ways." He laughed coldly, climbing like a roused lion to his feet beside Peter, and towered over him and the sheriff by nearly a full head.

"Skinner, you have always been trouble. You bring those half-broken wild mustangs to town for sale and then go helling around getting into fights. And there are a few other things I believe you're responsible for," hinted the sheriff darkly. He did not like having to look up at Skinner.

"But they are the best horses around and always bring premium prices," rebutted Skinner, while not being drawn into any discussion about the sheriff's second allegation. He turned and faced Peter. "If you don't mind, I'll drift along with you. I need to buy a shirt myself."

Pleased at the prospect of having Skinner's companionship, Peter smiled widely. "Be glad for your company." And they walked away, leaving the sheriff staring after them with a heavy scowl on his broad face.

CHAPTER 5

The powerful, multiscented aromas of the general store intoxicated Peter the moment he stepped through the door. He roamed about the building investigating a wonderful treasure house of familiar but mostly unfamiliar, strange and enticing items. His senses were overcome by the great variety of smells, and it took several minutes for them to begin to register as separate, individual odors.

He wandered about the shadowy aisles, inspecting their contents and recalling forgotten trips to other stores years before. For a long time he stood in front of the array of leather saddles, some with silver ornaments, most with high pommels, resting on wooden sawhorses. He picked an apple from one of the three barrels full of red and green early fall fruit near the center aisle and flashed it at the storekeeper to show him what he had and would pay for it later; teased his nose over the cheese rolls, large as fireplace wood, wrapped in heavy white cloth and stacked on a table along the cool north wall.

Peter passed without much hesitation the brightly colored bolts of cotton and velvet and the smaller rolls of lace and trim stacked behind the counter; lingered for a long time admiring a row of rifles and a lineup of pistols, all shiny with a protective coating of gun oil to prevent rusting. He tested his nose some more over the scads of items beyond quick count-ing, such as horehound candy, wild ginger, coal oil, horse-shoes, and Stetson hats.

With Skinner's guidance as to style and the storekeeper's help on size, Peter bought a complete complement of cloth-ing. To the purchase he added a large supply of ammunition for both his rifle and pistol, a packsaddle, a rain slicker, and two woollen blankets.

"Winter will soon be here," he observed to Skinner.

He paid with four gold coins, receiving change back. Bor-rowing a back-store room, he changed into the new outfit. Coming out, he piled his old clothes on the counter along with the remainder of his purchases.

The storekeeper wrapped it all in heavy paper. "Are you going to haul this in a wagon or on horseback?"

"On horseback," answered Peter.

The man pulled a burlap bag from under the counter and shoved the packages deep into the large, open mouth and tied it securely with strong twine. Peter made arrangements to leave it with the storekeeper until he would be ready to leave town and he and Skinner left the store.

"You said something about selling some cows tomorrow, so we should check to be sure the corral will be empty so you can use it," suggested Skinner.

"All right," Peter agreed, "but I want to get a haircut be-fore I leave town." They walked along the street to the far end of town where a large pole corral completely surrounded a low, rocky hill, a piece of ground that would not become muddy in wet weather.

"That's Old Gray!" exclaimed Peter, spotting a horse in-side the corral, and, running the last few steps, climbed nim-ble as a sun-warmed lizard up the pole fence and jumped down inside.

"I thought I had lost you for good, old boy," he laughed

happily, reaching out and running the long ears through his hands. The horse nickered and rubbed his big, intelligent head up and down Peter's chest.

"Hey, fellow, get away from my horse," ordered a harsh voice behind Peter.

"Your horse? But he is my horse. I lost him three days ago."

"He's been eating out of my feed bin for some time now. The damage is equal to his value, so I figure he is mine." Then shrewdly the man asked, "Let me see your bill of sale."

"What is a bill of sale?" asked Peter, feeling lost by the sudden claim on his horse. "The horse was my dad's and it naturally belongs to me now that he is dead."

Skinner heard the argument inside the corral and walked along the railing, tripped the wooden catch of the gate and entered. The man glanced at Skinner briefly, recognized him, and turned back to Peter.

A beauty, thought Skinner as he inspected the deep-chested, long-legged gray horse. A little past prime, maybe as much as twelve to fourteen years old, but nevertheless an outstanding piece of horseflesh. Just the kind a man would want when riding long and hard to save his neck.

"What's your brand then?" demanded the man, still arguing with Peter.

"Brand? There's no brand on this horse," said Peter in dismay, a slow swell of anger growing.

"Then you don't have any way to prove he's yours."

"But he is mine and no one is going to take him away from me." Peter quickly reached into his pocket and pulled out the change he had received from his recent purchase. "The most he could have been at your haystack is three days."

He looked down at the money, counted it, and held it out toward the hard-eyed man. "Here is six dollars—that should be plenty to pay you for all the feed he ate and your trouble tending him."

The man shook his head derisively and grinned at Skinner. "This kid is trying to buy a valuable horse for six dollars. Now ain't that dumb, Skinner?"

"Not as dumb as you are, Mac, if you try to keep his horse. Anybody can see the horse knows him, and I believe it's his."

"Are you taking sides, Skinner?"

"I don't have to," answered Skinner, smiling knowingly. "He is man enough to keep what is his. I suggest you take the six dollars and call it a good bargain."

"And if I don't?"

"Mac, I've seen you use a gun and you are just fair. My friend here is better, and he may not just scare you like he did the Fettuses, but take part of your hide. Some folks get angry at people trying to steal their horse."

Mac had heard the story of the Fettus brothers' run-in with a stranger and the results, somewhat embellished by the retelling. He looked at Peter and the well-used gun on his side with respect. "Skinner, if you think it is his horse, then I won't argue any more about it."

"That's fine, Mac. How about the use of the corral for a couple of hours tomorrow morning, early?"

"I reckon so. You want to sell some more horses?"

"Nope. Peter here wants to sell some cattle—maybe forty-five or fifty head. How much for that?"

"Two bucks."

"Does that sound all right to you, Peter?" asked Skinner.

"Sounds fair," replied Peter. "I'll be here with the cows a couple of hours after daylight."

"Now let's line up the cattle buyer," suggested Skinner.

Peter nodded and smiled happily as he led the horse out of the corral.

Reluctantly the last rays of the day's sunlight were forced up the mountainside by the dark shadows growing in the valley. Peter, his stomach full of food and his chair reared back and propped against the outside log wall of Skinner's cabin, felt relaxed. The mountain country, very similar to Lost Mountain, added a pleasant, protected feeling. From the cabin, nestling in the edge of a dense stand of juniper above town, he could see far down the valley and thought he could make out the smoke from the evening cook fire at the Manderfield ranch house.

During the last three days Peter believed he had made several friends, and without doubt he had created enemies. But overall he was pleased with his progress since he had left Lost Mountain. Skinner especially seemed a likable fellow, but he imagined that if it had been Skinner he had faced in the street, the outcome could very likely have been different.

After getting his horse from Mac, he and Skinner had located Morcom, the cattle buyer, and had arranged for the sale of the cattle. He had then gotten a haircut and a shave, with Skinner joining him in both. They ate a good steak dinner served by a big-bosomed woman that Skinner constantly joked with. Then Skinner showed him his cabin and was now leaning propped beside Peter against the cabin wall, thinking his own thoughts and silently gazing out across the shadow-filled valleys.

"Do you want me to keep calling you Skinner or do you have a first name?" asked Peter after a long, pleasant silence.

"Just call me Skinner; everybody does except for one person," answered Skinner, with a sad, remembering look in his eyes.

"Okay. What did you mean when you said you sold the best horses in the country?" asked Peter, remembering what the sheriff had said about Skinner and his wild horses.

"Yep. Out that way"—and Skinner waved his hand toward

the distant lower foothills—"there is a big valley I call Round Valley, surrounded by rimrock on three sides and the alkali on the fourth. In it there is a large herd of wild horses. Each summer, when water is scarce and they have only two or three water holes, I go there and trap fifty or sixty head. I've been doing it for twelve years or so. I make as much money in three or four months as most people do in a year."

"But if they are wild, aren't they kind of small, scrubby stuff? My dad told me that without man to breed them right, they usually don't amount to much."

"Your dad told you right. While I'm waiting on them to get thirsty enough to come into the trap, I go out and shoot any that don't measure up to what I want. I especially shoot a lot of stallions, leaving only the very best. You may not believe it, but after all these years, that herd of wild ones is as good as any tame stock any place around."

"You kill horses every year?"

"Yep, and because of the drought this year, I've had to kill about fifty animals. But that's not nearly as many as that first year when I started. In the beginning, after two or three years just catching whatever came into the trap from the big herd, and I mean a very big herd, I finally realized how I could make some good money each and every year if I could get the quality of horse people would pay high prices for. But to control the quality, I had to control the breeding and do it year after year. So, I decided to lay claim to all the horses in the valley and allow only certain studs that I would select do the breeding. When I really looked around—and remember I was no older than you are now—I also saw the range grass was grubbed right into the ground by too many horses and half the year the horses were on starvation rations.

"Right then and there the idea came to me as to how to handle the whole problem. I rode to town and went back out there with two saddlebags of bullets. I must have killed a hundred fifty horses that first year. I shot so many the coyotes got too fat to hunt for themselves and just followed me around in packs. After I would shoot a horse and start to ride away, fifteen or twenty coyotes would swarm around the carcass like flies around honey. A few times I saw signs of a wolf or mountain lion, but they never showed themselves like the coyotes.

"I shot the ugly horses without good form and shape and also a bunch of good-looking stuff, except they were too small for good riding stock. There were too many for the range and that made a lot of runts. So I thinned the whole herd down to where it was in balance with the grass. I also did away with a lot of sorrels. A big portion of the herd was browns, and I wanted a herd with more whites, blacks, and grays, because they sell good."

"Don't you feel bad about all that killing?"

"Sometimes. But you got to remember there were too many mustangs for the grass on the range, and they all do better now. And do you know what would have happened when one of those real bad winters with deep snow came? Well, about half of the herd would have died of starvation and the ones that would have survived would have been in real sorry condition come the spring.

"Now, usually I just kill twenty-five to thirty each year for being ugly, and that, plus the ones I sell, keeps the herd at the right size."

"If they are that good, it looks like someone else would trap them and all your work would be for nothing."

Skinner laughed. "A few fellows have tried that. And I didn't do anything that first time. They only took a few since they weren't very good at trapping horses. I just put the word out that in the future anyone catching wild horses in Round Valley would be doing so at their own risk. And just to make it halfway legal, I roped some mares and put my brand on them and turned them back loose in the herd. Then I had the herd marked as mine. Even now, once I have a horse trapped that I'm going to turn loose, I put my brand on it.

"The way I see it, my horse herd is like a homestead. You may not know about it, but there's a law which says that a man can lay claim to a hundred and sixty acres of land, and if he lives on it and raises crops, he can get to own it. Also, he can protect it against anybody that tries to take it away from him. I see my horses same as a homestead and the young horses as my crop and I have the right to protect it."

"Did it work?"

Skinner laughed shortly, his eyes hard and frosty in remembrance of the different times men had tried to take his horses. "After two years or so, most folks believed what I had said."

"What happened in that time to make them believe?"

"Seven wild-horse wranglers disappeared around Round Valley." The words came through his lips soft and slow. "I specially remember two men who went there thinking they were the toughest men around and bragging they would bring back a string of the best horses in the herd. They had enough guns to start a war. They never were seen again. Must have fallen on their guns or got kicked to death by a stallion." Only Skinner's lips smiled.

He did not tell Peter about the last man to trap some of his horses.

CHAPTER 6

French was Sanchez again, the big, strong-looking Mexican who had drifted into town a few days before and loafed in the shade in the afternoon. Though from Canada, he was a passable Mexican, with his dark skin, black hair, and large charcoal eyes. At the moment he lolled in the shadow of the high, false front of the funeral parlor across the street from the saloon in Westfall.

He wore tight broadcloth trousers patched on one knee; the once-decorative silver-thread embroidery at the top of the pockets and down the outside of the legs was tattered and torn. A big sombrero, the brim turned up all the way around, like the rim of a miner's gold pan, was tilted down over his face until he could barely see out from under it.

As part of his disguise he had removed his belt and holster and carried his gun hidden in the waist of his pants under the tails of a faded vest. A Mexican wearing a weapon would more than likely draw trouble from the gringos, and French wanted no disturbance that would foul up his scheme.

The front of the funeral parlor was a logical vantage place from which to observe and evaluate the goings-on of the town. And a natural place for a curious Mexican to sit idly in the shade and watch the gringo men go in and out of the saloon and other townspeople passing up and down the street on private errands.

Underneath his indolent, lazy posture he was tense and watchful because the time was very near for the kidnapping. He worried that maybe he should have grabbed the girl and just ridden out. But some feeling that the odds for escape would soon get better held him.

Luz Acosta had ridden in during the night and reported everything ready, and he was now shacked up in the Mexican section of town. Perrine and McClung had returned with a dozen horses, and using Shorty's expert knowledge of the terrain, French saw to it that the horses and men were in place, stationed at strategic, hidden positions along the escape route. All of the gang members and their captive would relay across the desert on fast horses, so rapidly no posse could stay within fifty miles of them.

The watchful, cautious Shorty worried French. Somehow he knew the little man was onto the fact that even if the mine and cattle business had been in full swing and money bulged the walls of the bank, French would still have changed their plans. Was Shorty also close to figuring out the rest of his plans?

Beth Manderfield had innocently altered the original plan the day she walked past and smiled at him in the joyful exuberance of youth, her round, blue eyes flashing and reddish-blond hair shining like new gold in the breeze. French was captured and possessed by her beauty. The old dream of returning to Canada rich and sporting a beautiful woman soared up from the depths where it had sunk after so many failures to accumulate either the money or a suitable woman. The desire flooded his mind and could not be rooted out.

He would need all the ransom they might collect to return home in style. But the men would not easily give up their shares. He just might have to kill them all, then make a cautious, rapid dash for home in the mountains of Saskatchewan, ahead of the winter storms. By spring the girl would be pregnant and convinced she must stay with him. It had to end that way. The plan was complete and absolutely no one and nothing would stop him.

French almost dozed off in the warm sun. He snapped awake to sudden, sharp attention as the heavy door of the bank, located across the street, banged shut.

A young man, carrying a bulging saddlebag tossed over one shoulder and a long-barreled pistol thrust forward at the ready, stood poised, tiger ready for fight, in front of the bank. French rose up on one elbow to see better.

At that one flicker of movement, caught by the corner of his eye, the gunman whirled and faced the Mexican, who froze into place. Tensely they watched each other for a moment.

Seeing no movement that threatened him, the man quickly holstered his gun and jumped across the sidewalk to his horse. He tossed the saddlebag over the horse's neck, grabbed the horn with both hands, and, without using the stirrup, jerked himself into the saddle.

He spurred and the horse lunged away down the street, the dust churning up in a great plume and chasing the racing horse like a giant, yellow tail.

A man holding a snow-white handkerchief to his nose and yelling in a voice coarse with fear and anger rushed out through the bank door. "Help, we've been robbed! The bank has been robbed! Somebody get the sheriff." Without waiting, he broke into a run, his feet thudding down the sidewalk, and burst into the lawman's office a short block away.

Almost immediately the sheriff hurried out, the banker tagging at his heels, talking rapidly. They both stopped at the door of the saloon.

"Hey in there! The bank has been held up by Nate Pipe's

kid! Posse forming in five minutes. Get your guns and horses. Anyone else you run into, bring them along, too."

The sheriff hastened away toward the stable to get his own horse, stopping briefly at the general store and barbershop to again yell directions inside for the forming of the posse.

A half-dozen men slammed open the batwing doors of the saloon and scattered eagerly for their horses. Two men passed close by French at a trot.

"Damn! Finally something to do other than stand around and drink beer," chuckled one.

"Hell, I had six hundred dollars in the bank. How much do you suppose he got?"

"I don't know. Don't worry about it. We'll ride him down and get it all back."

The sheriff rode up in front of his office astride a long-legged bay that pranced and tossed his head in anticipation. The lawman glanced at the Mexican on the sidewalk but made no motion of invitation for him to join the hunt. Other horsemen swarmed in from several directions, some with rifles in scabbards under their legs while a few carried them in their hands as if they couldn't wait to shoot at something.

The contagious excitement of the men infected the horses, and they milled, pawed the ground, and jostled each other. One put his head down and made a few stiff-legged bucking jumps down the street. The rider yanked his head up and hit him over the ears with his hat a few times to get him under control.

"All right," shouted the sheriff above the noise, "we'll try and catch him before dark. If we don't find him today, it could be a long trail and then we'll take packhorses and supplies and run him to ground. I mean to get him. Anyone who can't keep up will be left behind. So don't come unless you got a good horse.

"Jamison, that crowbait you got ain't good enough to keep

up, so you stay in town. Jallapi, how about that sorry thing you're riding?"

"Hell, Sheriff, I'll be right there when you catch him."

"Let's go then. He already has a two-mile start on us." The sheriff let out a piercing yell, jerked his hat off and swung it in a long overhand sweep down the street the way the bank robber had fled. He spurred into a dead run.

The remainder of the hunters surged forward onto the chase after the lawman, the riders in the rear trying to jockey forward in the pack to escape the fog of dust. The clatter of hoofbeats darted and echoed along the street, finally working their way to the edge of town and dying out against the side of the mountain.

French stood up quickly as the last of the pursuing horsemen vanished down over the hill from town. The roiled dust settled back to the dry ground and onto the porches of the houses lining the street. The town lay quiet and defenseless.

This was the perfect situation he had been waiting for. The law and nearly a dozen guns were gone.

He laughed low and savage. "I've got you now, Beth Manderfield." And he hurried along the street to the Mexican section of town to find Acosta and their horses.

Shaking a noonday nap from heavy eyelids, John Manderfield stepped out through the arched stone doorway of his house into the yard. After the dark interior of the house, he had to squint his eyes to see through the blinding sunlight. He saw Peter's gray horse tied to the hitching rail. Knowing Peter's preference for the roan, he wondered why the gray was there. Then he saw the pack on its back.

He crossed the yard and opened the flaps of the pack to find a bedroll, slicker, grub, canteens of water, and ammunition, plenty for a long trip. Puzzled as to why Peter had said nothing about leaving, John started back to the house to question him.

As he crossed the yard, a puff of dust scurrying along the road from town caught his eye. Rapidly it swept toward him, and a faint mutter of hoofbeats grew gradually stronger. The dust cloud drew nearer and the dark shape of a rider and running horse grew visible, framed against it. He made out the now familiar form of Peter, leaning forward over the horse's neck, riding easily to the fast gait.

In the very early morning that day, he and Peter had driven the young man's livestock to town and sold them to the cattle buyer. Peter had pocketed the bank draft for $1,500 with a disappointed frown on his face.

"A long way from nine or ten thousand dollars," he observed dryly.

"Yes, but a good start towards a ranch of your own," answered John.

"A very poor start. It will take me years to earn the rest of the money."

"I have known many men die old after working their whole lives away and not have as much cash money as you do now," replied John.

"What other men didn't have won't buy me a ranch," responded Peter.

John realized Peter would not be easily changed, so he shifted subjects. "Why don't you put the money in the bank for safe keeping?"

"That sounds like a good idea."

John sat down on the bench in front of the bank and waited in the early morning sun while Peter was inside. Peter had received a fair price for his cattle and should have been more pleased.

Peter came out of the bank in a very short time. "I've decided not to give them my money. I had the money draft made into cash and I'll just keep it on me."

John was surprised at Peter's decision not to deposit the money, but said nothing. They rode back to the ranch in almost complete silence. John's efforts to start a conversation were responded to only briefly by the reflective young man, and it grew obvious he did not want to talk. Once at the ranch they separated, each tending to his own needs.

But now John realized Peter must have packed his horse and returned to town almost immediately.

Peter closed the distance rapidly, riding almost up against the yard fence before he dragged the horse to a sliding stop. Excited and caught up in the stimulation of the race, the horse fought the bit, tossing his head and dancing sideways for a moment before Peter could calm him down with some gentle words and a few pats on the neck.

The boy's finely chiseled features were strained and his eyes large and restless as he worked the roan up beside the gray and jerked the lead rope loose.

"What's wrong, Peter?" asked John in a quick, worried voice.

"I just robbed the bank to get the other eight thousand dollars I need to buy me a ranch," Peter answered tersely.

"What did you say?" John could not believe what he had heard.

"I held up the bank!"

"Why, for God's sake, did you do that?"

"My dad told me that if I ever needed money to just rob a bank."

"Boy, surely he did not mean that," said John, a deep feeling of apprehension for Peter settling in the pit of his stomach.

"He said it. I heard it plain as anything, and he said if you could get away from the sheriff, you got to keep it."

"But he must have been joking with you."

"He wasn't smiling; he was serious," responded Peter, remembering the ironic, sad face of his wounded and dying father lying in the cabin on the mountain.

"I still think he did not mean it—he couldn't have. You were his son, and he must have known it was wrong and could only lead you to trouble."

"Yes, he meant it. Everything he told me has come out right. I got to be going. The sheriff will be close behind me."

John reached out quickly and grabbed the bridle of the horse to hold Peter so he could talk with him. "Did you hurt anyone?"

"No!"

"Then give the money back. I will explain it to them; explain why you took the money."

"No, I must keep it for my ranch." Peter yanked the horse's head free from the old man's feeble hand.

Spurring the roan, he sped down the trail, following the valley bottom toward the alkali-filled playa. The gray horse, towed along, tried to match strides and keep up to relieve the pressure of the jerking rope cutting into his neck.

John watched helplessly as Peter disappeared, the brown horse sprinting and the gray scampering along behind and one step to the right to stay clear of the flying hooves.

How had one man pulled off the robbery in the middle of the day without getting caught? John checked the road leading toward town. Sure enough, a knot of hard-riding horsemen were already close enough to begin to separate into individual riders.

They turned off the main road, climbed the bluff to the house, and swirled up to let their horses surround the old man.

"John, did that Pipe kid pass here?" called the sheriff, a little out of breath and having to raise his voice above the noisy riders and horses.

John nodded his white head in the affirmative.

"Where is he heading?"

"I don't know."

"Listen, John, you and I have known each other for years and have always been square in our dealings. Now, tell me quick what you know about where he might be going. We've got to be riding."

"Gumert, he is just a kid and not used to our rules." John was very afraid for Peter; the sheriff was an expert and dogged tracker.

"Well, everybody knows you don't rob banks."

"Tell me, Sheriff, how did a kid hold up a bank so easily in daylight, right in the center of town?" John hoped to gain time for Peter.

"Just pure luck," answered the sheriff. "He caught one of the tellers gone to lunch and the banker out back at the well soaking his head trying to stop one of his damn nosebleeds. Only that new teller Gardner was inside and he just loaded Pipe's saddlebags up with eight thousand dollars when Pipe pulled his gun and told him to."

"Gumert, you and I both know who his parents were, and he thinks his father told him to rob a bank when he needed money."

"Well, we'll teach him a lesson he won't soon forget. Did he take an extra horse with him?"

"Yes."

"And supplies?"

"Yes."

"Then loan us some grub and water. This may be a longer chase than I first thought."

The riders hurriedly filled canteens. Yolanda and Miguel packed food and blankets. Two extra horses carrying packsaddles were brought up to the back door and the supplies loaded. In a hard, vengeful mood like a pack of hunting dogs, the heavily armed and provisioned posse thundered out of the yard. Their dust cloud rose and hung in the air for a long time, pointing straight along Peter's exact route.

As John stood watching the posse's dust settle, two large Mexicans, riding long-legged, deep-chested horses turned up the slope toward the house. They reined in very close to him and the one on the left gave a friendly smile.

"*Buenos días,* señor," he said, touching his hat in salute. In heavily Spanish-accented English he continued, "Is that the dust of the posse I see that way?" And he pointed to the string of dust stretching far down the valley.

John nodded once.

"Then our timing is just right," he said as he swung down from his mount.

"I did not ask you to step down," said John, bristling at the man's effrontery in dismounting without being invited.

The man ignored John. "Cover him, Luz, while I get the girl," he ordered and started toward the house.

The man called Luz threw his leg quickly over the saddle, kicked free, and slid to the ground. As he landed he pulled his handgun from its holster and pointed it at John.

"Do not move or I will shoot you," he threatened.

"What's going on? What do you want with Beth?" demanded John.

"Is she as pretty as they say?" asked Luz, paying no attention to John's question.

"Damn you, tell me what's going on."

"We're taking your granddaughter on a nice long ride while you get *mucho dinero* for us to get her back." He smiled showing broken yellow teeth, and his eyes mocked John. "Maybe I should have said 'get her back safe.'"

A pistol shot roared inside the house and the window in the stone walls rattled. Beth's shrill cry of terror pierced John and he spun around to face in the direction of its source. The scream cut off abruptly at the top of its crescendo.

John lunged toward the house to help his granddaughter. The younger man sprang forward and intercepted him, grabbed a handful of the shirt covering John's scrawny chest, and shook him savagely. "Now don't do anything loco—I don't want you dead."

John clenched his hand into a hard fist and struck the threatening face, the bony knuckles smashing squarely on the big nose. Bright red blood streamed from inside each nostril and, like two crimson springs, washed down across the coarse lips, soaking the whiskered chin and dribbling onto the dirty shirt.

The big fist holding John's shirt jerked him forward and rammed him backward, repeating it again and again, the rock-hard knuckles almost shattering the ancient chest bones. The weight of the flopping head, whipped back and forth by the sudden changes in direction, strained the thin, spindly neck to the verge of snapping it.

Pain ripped through John's chest and sharp, jaggered spears of yellow and white rushed across his vision followed by blackness. He clutched at the big hand holding him and let his full weight ride on it to stop its beating of him. No good to Beth dead, he reasoned, and fought his mind back toward full consciousness.

The murderous face of Luz swam back into the focus of John's hate-filled eyes. "I will kill you," the old man promised.

Luz's foul breath assaulting John, the outlaw ruthlessly stabbed his pistol barrel against his head at the temple and ground and twisted the hard steel into the soft spot until the old man thought his mind would explode with the searing pain. And the pain went on and on.

"If we didn't need you, I'd blast your brains all over this yard," hissed the bandit.

"Ease up there, you dumb Mexican! Do you want to kill him?" yelled French from the doorway. He hurried down the path to the fence, dragging Beth, stumbling and half falling behind him.

Luz reluctantly slackened the pressure of the gun barrel.

"Took a little while to get her into riding clothes," said French. He grinned.

Beth was dazed and her large eyes were glazed and uncomprehending. A large, ugly, rose-colored bruise, where French had struck her, swelled and distorted the side of her face. She was dressed in boots, tight-legged pants, and heavy cotton shirt; a wide-brimmed hat on a leather thong around her neck hung down her back.

French saw the blood on Luz's face and chuckled. "Rough old rascal, ain't he?"

"What was the shot for?" asked Luz.

"I had to shoot the fat man. He thought I shouldn't take the girl and tried to stop me. Saddle her a good horse and I'll tell Grandpa here what he's got to do."

Luz released his hold on John, wiped his nose on his sleeve, and stalked off toward the corrals.

"Now, listen carefully," French said. "I'm taking the girl with me and whether or not she returns safe to you depends on you doing exactly as I say, and I mean everything exactly as I say." His cruel eyes bored into John. "Sometime within the next five to seven days, you will get a message from me saying where you're to deliver seventy-five thousand dollars in cash."

"God, man, I don't have that kind of money. There is no way I can do it."

"Just shut up and listen. I know you are worth it, so don't leave fifty or sixty thousand. You leave the full seventy-five thousand, every penny, and make it gold and no paper-money bills over a hundred dollars. You ride to Brogan right now and catch the night train to Denver. When you get there, go to the main branch of the Merchant's and Cattleman's Bank. Be sure you have papers showing who you are and a draft from the bank here in Westfall so you can draw out the money. Come back here immediately and wait. And for your granddaughter's sake, keep your mouth shut."

"I wish I had a gun."

"Old man, even if you had a gun, it wouldn't do you any good. Get it through your thick head you got to do as I say. This is a mighty pretty girl"—he pulled Beth up tight against his body—"a beautiful girl, and you don't want me to turn her over to six or seven men for a plaything, do you?"

"I'll—I'll do the best I can. Please don't hurt her. Where do you want me to deliver the money?"

"I told you, you would be told that when you return. Don't miss today's train or you might end up a day too late and never see your granddaughter again." Deep within the recesses of his mind, French knew she would never be seen again in this land.

Luz rode up and swung a spare horse in beside French and Beth.

"They sure have good-looking horses here. Want to take some extra ones?"

"No time. They'd just get in the way. We're going to follow the plan as we laid it out."

French slipped his hands up under Beth's arms and easily hoisted her astride her mount. Quickly he adjusted the stirrups to her leg length and mounted his own horse.

"You get on your way, old man, and right now," ordered French.

He spurred away, leading Beth's horse, the girl hanging on to the pommel. Luz brought up the rear, glancing back once to see John hurrying to the house.

John hammered on the thick, wooden door of Skinner's cabin with his fist, ramming and rattling it against the latch and hinges inside.

"Skinner, this is John Manderfield. I've got to talk with you, right now."

He waited a moment in silence, but there was no reply from inside.

"Damn you, Skinner, I know you are in there. Answer me!"

He drew back his heavy boot and kicked the rough planking of the door with fierce energy. The door opened a crack as the nail holding the latch was driven part way out of the door casing.

"Manderfield, you old bastard, I don't want to talk with you. Get off my land. If I come out there, I'm going to thrash your old hide. Now go away."

"I've already been beaten up, and it's Beth that needs help. Come out, please!"

Almost instantly the door was jerked open, and Skinner stood blinking whiskey-reddened eyes in the bright afternoon sun.

"What's happened to Beth?"

"About an hour ago two men kidnapped her," answered John, then stopped when he saw the blank look in the big man's eyes. "Are you sober enough to understand what I'm saying?"

"I understand," and the blue eyes focused with savage intensity on John's face. "Tell me all of it."

"The sheriff had just been gone for a few minutes when those two Mexicans rode up. I don't believe one was a Mex, just acting . . ."

Skinner interrupted John with an impatient swing of a muscular arm. "Tell it all, man—all of it."

"All right, all right. About noon Peter robbed the bank of eight thousand dollars and took off across the desert, probably going back to Lost Mountain. He came by my place to get his other horse and supplies he had packed on him. Just a few minutes later the sheriff rides up with a posse. He tried to get me to tell him where Peter went. And since I didn't know, I couldn't tell him anything. The posse got grub and pack animals from me and they left, hot after Peter. The Fettus brothers were riding with the sheriff.

"Those two Mexicans must have been waiting for something like this that would take the law away," continued John, describing the remainder of the past events. "There must be a gang of them, for this one fellow who acted like the leader threatened to turn Beth over to seven men if I didn't pay them the money."

Skinner's eyes were frosty and the freckles on his skin were a swarm of brown bugs plastered on the pale, taut face. He stepped a pace closer to John.

"What is it you want?"

John knew Skinner was forcing him to say it. "I want you to go after them and bring her back. You are the best tracker and rifle shot anywhere around. I want them dead and Beth safe at home."

Skinner grinned ironically. "You want me to track down and kill several men and bring back a girl you refused to let me court? You remember you said I was too old for her and was a drunk and good-for-nothing?"

"I remember all that," admitted John.

"If I bring her back, I'm going to try to get her to marry me," stated Skinner, locking eyes with the old man.

"She will make her own decision this time," agreed John, "if we get her back. Do you think you can catch them?"

"Sure, if they stay together and I have enough time. If they split up and travel a long distance straight away, I'll not catch them. But I figure they will stick together until they get the ransom money. But it will take me a while to come on to them. They will have staked out horses and supplies and be able to move much faster than I can. I'll have only a couple of horses, and when they get rode down, I'll just have to stop and rest them."

"Let's hope they make a mistake," said John.

"If they don't, I won't overtake them. Now, I've got to get some supplies together. Go around back to the corral and saddle the stallion for me. There is a mare and colt in with him. Put the pack hanging in the shed on her and a long lead rope."

"Why take the mare? I'll buy you the best riding horse in town. Just pick it out."

"I don't have time to explain. Do what I ask. The mare is tough—one of the wild ones I brought in last time."

While John readied the horses, Skinner piled a small mound of hunting necessities in the doorway. As an afterthought he tossed his telescope onto the heap.

Skinner looked out across the town and beyond to the desert. For the first time in several months gray-white thunderheads were piling and building in the northwest. He hoped it did not rain and wash out the tracks.

He and Manderfield mounted and rode at a fast pace toward town.

They pulled their horses up in front of the unpainted livery stable.

"Have them take care of the colt. It is near enough weaned to be without the mare's milk, but see if they can find a little cow's milk for a few days."

"I'll take care of it," promised John. "Good hunting."

"You know, considering how much I am out gunned, they may kill me instead of me getting them."

"I know. They killed Miguel easy enough. But you are not Miguel."

Skinner did not acknowledge the compliment. "Do exactly what they told you to. Catch that train from Brogan tonight and get back as quick as you can with the money."

"I plan to do just that."

Skinner reined away down the street leading the mare. She tugged back against the rope and nickered plaintively at her colt, being held in check by John's arm around its neck. Skinner jerked on the mare's lead rope to get her attention, touched the stallion with his spurs, and they picked up the pace as they left town.

CHAPTER 7

The lone golden eagle flew high and straight, his long, powerful wings rhythmically pumping him across the alkali desert. He spotted the lone rider and his two horses and looked them over, but other than that, the desolate gray expanse held no interest for him. It was only a lifeless chunk of land to cross to get to his late summer hunting territory.

Peter Pipe watched the brown body beat its way across the opal sky, passing overhead and then growing smaller and disappearing in the south. Beneath the baking sun, Lost Mountain appeared to shiver and twist, its form contorted by the layers of hot air pouring from the scorching earth. Peter ignored the distortions created by the rising heated air and cut straight across in the direction of the north end of the mountain. He did not follow his previous route, for he planned to stay well clear of his cabin.

As he rode along, his mind kept returning to John Manderfield's comments that he had misunderstood his father's advice and it was wrong to rob a bank. He reached back to where the saddlebags were tied and felt their bulging leather sides. A sickening fear grew in him that he had made a great mistake.

Having settled into the monotonous routine of travel across the unchanging landscape, the horses, except to be repointed toward Lost Mountain now and then, required little attention. Only the soft scuff of their hooves, as Peter alternately trotted and walked them, broke the silence. Their iron-shod feet left half-circle imprints in the puffed-up bentonite clay and alkali soil.

Peter, from time to time, searched the desert behind him, but could not yet discover any pursuers. He dozed off and on as the almost perfectly flat land slid smoothly beneath the horse's belly and the mountain grew and took on familiar, intimate detail with each passing hour.

In the evolution of the land, the mountain was young and reared up out of the desert at an abrupt and untouched angle. Peter reached it in the evening and, picking the most gentle slope though still a steep one, began to climb. He pulled his map out again and checked the array of symbols showing the mountain, arroyos, and what he was searching for, the spring. It was hidden in a small, deep crevice, a thousand feet above the desert floor, but with the expert craftsmanship of the map, he found it fairly easily.

No one would have suspected the spring to be there. But inside the lava rock of the mountain, the water, ever seeking the lowest elevation, found its way down through the secret channels, cracks, and porous cinders. It gurgled out of the black rock, dripped in a steady stream, big as his little finger, onto the ground, moistening a narrow green ribbon of grass the length of a lariat and vanishing into the brown sand of the bottom of the wash. The evenly spaced, precisely aligned, round pad marks of a bobcat in the sand were the only signs of life he saw.

Peter made twenty trips, carrying his hat full of water up over the rocks from the arroyo bottom. He took turns, holding the approximately one gallon of water, for first one horse, then the other. They drank with deep, sucking noises, their nostrils often buried in the water; and when they lifted their heads to breathe, they sometimes snorted out the liquid, spraying Peter. He laughed, for on this blistering day it felt good on his hot skin.

Dehydrated by the long, hot trek, the horses drank nearly ten gallons apiece. When they had all they wanted, Peter filled his two canteens.

If the posse could not find the water hole, it would surely be slowed down, reasoned Peter. So he led the horses back down the mountainside a hundred yards or so along the trail he had used to climb to the spring. Then he broke off a sagebrush limb and brushed away all imprints left in the dirt by himself and the animals between the spring and where the horses were now tied.

He climbed aboard the roan and reached down and smoothed away the last of his boot prints. Critically he examined his efforts to trick his pursuers. The trail from the desert where he had come up and around the flank of the mountain lay easy to follow. And he would make the trail equally visible as he rode on. Satisfied he would not be tracked to the spring, he resumed his journey. At a steep ledge he tossed the used limb of the sagebrush over the side so it would not be found.

On the most northerly point of the mountain he stopped and his eyes searched back the long way he had come. As the afternoon had spent itself, the heat had diminished; the distortion of view present early in the day was gone and he could see several miles. No living thing moved on the desert.

He dismounted, loosened the cinches on the horses and tied up their reins and lead rope so they would not trip over them, and then let the two animals graze on the dry bunch grass. The horses liked his company and would not stray more than a few yards. He found a comfortable lookout and rested and dozed.

Peter awakened with the dusk of the evening already slipping silently across the desert from the east. Somewhat surprised by the rapid passage of time while he slept, he stood up quickly. Sure enough the posse was there, not three miles away, the knot of riders sniffing along his trail like a big black spider.

At his first whistle the roan lifted his head, holding a long tuft of grass between his big teeth, and looked at him. On the second blast he obediently trotted to Peter, the gray horse following close behind. Peter exchanged the saddle and pack between horses and climbed up on the gray. In short order he was down off the mountainside and heading west, beginning the crossing of the second half of the ancient lake bottom.

The crescent of the moon, thin as a single curved, silver thread, rose in the east. As the darkness caught up with and overrode Peter, the stars came out reluctantly, one by one. The grayness of the early night soon gave way to black gloom. Peter looked for and found the Big Dipper and the North Star. Together they made a giant celestial clock—the diamond-studded Big Dipper pivoting around the less noticeable North Star would mark each passing hour and also be his guide through the dark night.

He was glad for the weak moon. The sheriff and his hunters would be forced to lay up until daylight. Peter smiled into the helpful darkness, and for awhile the beauty of the night overcame his dread of the mistake he might have made in robbing the bank.

All things of the desert were hushed and silent. Peter dreamed of pretty Beth's laugh and the things she talked about, and of the gaunt old man trying to hold his horse by the bridle and tell him something important. The eyes pleaded for him to listen and the lips moved, and though Peter listened intently, he could not make out what the man was saying.

He drifted awake surrounded by complete darkness. The

tired horses stood motionless, resting. A ghostly night flyer drifted past almost soundless, not a foot from his head, the wings fluttering ever so slightly as it maintained its course. It returned to investigate, diving down to brush the brim of his hat, and then up and away into the darkness and did not return.

Reluctant to disturb the silence, Peter sat and rested with the horses. A puff of night wind slipped in out of the blackness and caressed his face. The gray spread his ears as if he had heard something, then relaxed again. But the spell was broken and Peter clucked him into motion to the west. Though he could see little, he read the feelings of the horses and the signals their ears and heads made against the lighter gray of the ground.

He rode through the night, the Big Dipper marking off the hours.

"Damn it, I know the little bastard found water up there," cursed the sheriff. "Why else would he have climbed up over that high country?"

The posse had felt its dangerous way down the steep slope of the mountain in the darkness. Now on the flat, amid the creak of leather and jingle of metal from the movements of the horses and men, they considered their next step.

"Should we go back up on foot and try to find it tonight or wait till morning?" someone asked.

"Neither," answered the sheriff. "I know of water across on the other side and about four or five miles back in the hills from the alkali."

"Yeh, I know where that spring is, too," said a voice from out of the tangle of men.

"Maybe there is water in the hills, but add that to the distance we still have to go on the flat and that adds up to thirty or thirty-five miles to go without water," cautioned another voice from the blackness.

"Does anyone have good enough night eyes to make out the trail right now?" asked the sheriff, almost completely blind in the darkness.

"I can," said a young voice from near the west side of the group.

"You can see it good enough to lead us?"

"Sure can, Sheriff. The hoof marks are squashed down in the inside and ridged up on the outside rim and are darker than the rest of the ground. They don't call me Eagle Eye for nothing," he said and chuckled.

"Then let's move out. We'll rest later on, but I want to be in the hills before daylight. I still plan to catch that fellow," said the sheriff. "Who said he also knew where that spring is? What's your name?"

"It's me, Sheriff, Jake Jallapi."

"All right, help me keep the direction to it straight, and if this track angles off too much, we'll leave it and come back and hunt it up after we water down."

Following the nearly invisible form of the young horseman, the other riders lined out through the deep murk under the splinter of moon.

Ollie Fettus rode last in line. He leaned forward toward his brothers riding immediately ahead in the darkness. "Hey, Buck, and you, too, Oscar, hold up a minute."

The two brothers briefly reined in their mounts and Ollie squeezed his steed in between them. He reached out with his long arms, hooked them around the necks of the two younger members of his family and pulled them partway to him.

"Listen good. The very first second we get the chance, we shoot Pipe," he said in a low, hate-filled whisper.

"Ollie, the sheriff won't like that," answered Buck.

"I don't give a damn what Gumert likes. We're sworn-in

deputies now and part of the law. Get your rifles out fast and cut him down. They won't do anything after it's over," his voice hissed.

They rode along a few paces in silence. Ollie felt the stiff necks of his brothers against his arms. The sheriff was a hard and dangerous man when crossed and they all knew it.

"The sheriff don't like Pipe, either. I think he wouldn't mind him dead," continued Ollie.

Ollie contracted his arms, putting pressure on the two men. "Well, what do you say? Do you agree?"

"I'm with you," answered Buck in a low voice. "I didn't like him showing us up like he did in town that day."

"Yeh, me, too," agreed Oscar, "but I think we are all going to get into big trouble."

"It will come out all right," assured Ollie. "Say, can't you fellows see the trail clear enough to follow?"

They both answered that they could.

"Then the sheriff must be losing his eyesight in his old age," laughed Ollie. "We got to keep that in mind. Now let's catch up."

John Manderfield was light-headed and dizzy as he pulled his horse to a stop at the hitching rail in the center of Brogan. The long ride from Westfall had strained him badly.

In the wall of the one-story stone building directly in front of him, a heavy plank door stood open, and above the shadowy entrance hung an old wooden sign spelling out SHERIFF, BROGAN COUNTY, OREGON. Though he had seen the sign many times before, he could barely make it out, for it and the doorway seemed to swing back and forth as if hanging on the end of a piece of string. He remained astride the horse in the evening sun and waited for the light-headedness to pass, watching the door swing like a pendulum. He touched the bank draft in his pocket. He had had to mortgage his ranch and his interest in the mine at Silver City to the hilt to obtain the necessary ransom money.

The giddiness still persisted after two or three minutes so he climbed down, but that made it worse and he clung to the pommel and leaned his head against the sweaty leather of the saddle. A man, walking along the sidewalk, hesitated and looked at him, then continued on his way without offering to help.

John raised his eyes and measured the distance to the door. He thought he could make it. Taking slow, careful steps, he crossed the few feet and stepped inside.

"John Manderfield, what in blue blazes brings you all the way to Brogan on a day like this?" asked Sheriff Tim Matlock, quickly getting up from behind an ancient wooden desk and circling around it to shake John's hand.

The old man staggered and the sheriff thrust out his big hands, grabbed the frail shoulders, and eased him onto a chair. He pulled another chair up close and sat down, ready to support his longtime friend if he needed it.

"You sit there and rest and tell me what the trouble is," said Matlock. He looked at the bowed gray head with the chin resting on the thin chest and recalled the first time he had seen John. That had been somewhere around twenty-five years ago when as a young man he had ridden to the Manderfield ranch in search of his first job.

While waiting for an opportunity to ask Manderfield for the job, Tim stood near a set of corrals and watched the rancher, vigorous and smiling, branding the calves with the help of two hired hands. Manderfield, riding a black roping horse, selected a calf from a clutter of them in the far end of the corral and took out after it, his rope twirling above his head. He was good at it, the lariat flying true. The instant the calf hit the end of the rope and went down, the horse began to back slowly, keeping the calf dragging along just enough to keep it from getting to its feet. One of the cowboys snatched a hot branding iron from the fire and ran forward. He pressed a heavy knee on the calf's shoulder to hold it still, shoved the searing iron against the hairy skin, rocked it just a tiny bit to make sure the tips of the brand came out distinct, jerked it away from the burned, bawling calf, loosened the loop of the rope, tossed it free, and dashed back to plunge the cooled iron into the hot coals of the fire.

"That took you all of seven seconds," John chided the man with the branding iron. "You got to do better than that to work for me." John's laughter mixed with the dust as he whirled his horse away. "Let's try for six seconds on the next one," he yelled over his shoulder as he jerked the loop to himself, shook it out to a larger size, and sped away after another fleet-footed calf.

Tim had gotten the job and worked for John for six years, and often they had beat seven seconds.

The old man raised his faded blue eyes and looked at the sheriff. "I can't tell you what the trouble is, Tim, not yet. But I got to be on the evening train to Denver."

"John, you know I'd bust a gut to do everything I could to help you," said Tim, "and I'll see that you are on that train."

John nodded his agreement to the declaration of help. "Another thing, I'm going to be bringing a lot of money—seventy-five thousand dollars—when I come back. Do you have anyone who can go with me? A deputy maybe, to act as guard?"

"Better than that. I'll go with you myself. I could stand a trip to the big town."

"I was hoping you'd say that. Now that that's settled, may I borrow some paper and a pencil?"

"Sure, just a minute." Tim went behind the desk and dug a few sheets of paper from the desk drawer and a stub of a lead pencil. "Here, let me help you over to my chair so you can write on the desk top."

John wrote slowly for nearly five minutes. Then he folded the two sheets of paper and put them in his shirt pocket.

"Do you want me to get the doctor for you?" asked Tim, still concerned at John's appearance.

"No time for a doctor. What we've got to do is more important than me. But I would like to lay down until about time for the train."

"Use my bunk over there. And while you are resting, I'll take your horse to the livery and go get our tickets for the train."

John walked to the bed and sat down. "Tim, remember we've got to get the money. You see that I get to the bank in Denver even if you have to carry me."

Tim looked piercingly at John. "It's Beth that's in trouble, ain't it? Are you sure you don't want me to do something? I can have a posse of a dozen men in five minutes."

"Not now. I've just got to get to Denver. If something happens to me, please do what I've written out right here in my pocket."

"Okay, have it your way." Tim turned to leave.

"Tim, I'm asking you as a friend and sheriff to do it exactly as I have it written. Do you agree?"

"I'll do it as you say. But let me tell you something: if Beth is hurt in any way, I'll take care of those who did it, I promise that, too." He stomped out.

CHAPTER 8

"The sun's almost up," called French. "Let's mount up and ride." He stepped into the saddle and, turning, surveyed the camp and the other members of the band. His eyes stopped and came to rest on Beth, her riding pants tightening and caressing the flare of her woman's hips as she lifted her foot into the stirrup and pulled herself astride.

Beth was only slightly sore as they loped out of camp at a fast pace. She had always ridden a moderate amount and credited her ability to stand up under the first day's hard riding to that. The swollen place on the side of her face where French had slugged her was mostly gone. But it was an ugly black and blue, like a half-rotten plum, and tender when she touched it.

The gang pushed rapidly across the dry land on fresh horses. Shorty and Storms had met the kidnappers and their captive with the first relay of horses and several gallons of water the evening before. The two heavily armed men had watched the three approach for a long distance from a high lookout and were ready to assist in the event a posse had been close. But there was no sign of pursuit and they rode down to the rendezvous point to meet with French in the gray darkness of early night.

Storms had prepared supper for the tired riders and Shorty

led the exhausted horses off a couple of miles and scattered them to fend for themselves. After watching them work their way south along some old horse trails until they would not be found and used by someone trailing them, he had returned to camp.

Throughout the morning hours, Beth kept up with the other riders and did not complain. The men, without any visible plan, and apparently at random, seemed to always surround her. She measured their horses—as first one and then another rode beside her—and decided she had been given the least strong and slowest animal of the bunch. She knew it was a deliberate move to give her little chance to break away from the outlaw band.

One by one, Beth caught the eyes of a captor and tried to decide whether he would be a friend or enemy if she ever called on him for help. She was dismayed by what she saw, for to her young woman's view, the eyes appeared without compassion, lustful, examining her as a stud would a mare he was waiting on to come into heat. But French was the worst of the lot; his penetrating, raping looks almost made her shudder.

She had not yet found the eye of the oldest man, the one they called Shorty. Once she did catch the tail end of his look as he turned away, but not enough to detect any indication of his thoughts.

These men were outcast and not bound or governed by the rules of other people. She had to escape or acquire a protector. And at all times keep as many of them around her as possible, hoping there would be safety in numbers.

As the group topped out on the high rise, Beth looked back quickly along their trail, searching for anyone tracking them.

"Forget it. There ain't anybody close enough for you to see them," said French, a satisfied smirk on his face.

She did not answer, looking again to the front. He was correct. The rested horses and cached water that had been waiting for them the evening before had given the gang a tremendous advantage. Anybody following must surely detour to find water, and their horses would wear down and be far behind.

Her grandfather would not be one of those searching for her, she reasoned. He was too ill for that. The sheriff with a posse might possibly be trailing, but her grandfather had told her a posse was a slow, clumsy critter and if made up of town men, would soon give up the chase. If all that were true, it was very unlikely that a posse would catch such an organized group of bandits.

Then all of a sudden Beth remembered John Skinner, and his face flashed pleasantly into her mind. Yes, he would be the one to keep the trail, hang on grimly until he found her. In her wholehearted belief she smiled, a small flash of her white teeth showing between her lips.

"What's so damn funny?" asked French, his ever-watchful eyes having noticed the faint smile.

Beth did not answer. Hastily she controlled her expression and continued to look straight ahead at the back of Shorty, riding in front of her. But she continued to think of John Skinner.

Skinner's father and John Manderfield had come to the high desert country of Oregon together. Skinner named his only son after his friend. While Manderfield accumulated property and wealth, the elder Skinner trapped wild mustangs and searched for gold. His son grew up, always out in the mountains or the desert with his father.

During their trips to town, the Skinners often stayed at the Manderfield ranch. Then one day young John came in from the desert without his father and sat in the house of Manderfield and cried as he told of his father's horse falling and throwing him, cracking his head on the black lava rocks.

Manderfield had a very personal sorrow at this same time. His widowed son had died, caught and crushed in a cave-in at the mine his father partially owned. On the living-room floor a small, golden-haired girl toddled about. She went toward the young man and reaching up, clutched at his dusty trousers, staring up into his face. She reached up and touched the glistening tears on his tanned cheeks. As children do, her tiny fingers quickly deposited the shiny liquid onto her tongue and she tasted and savored the mildly salty flavor. Even today she could still remember the smell and taste of him.

Young John continued to visit at the Manderfield ranch, maybe even more than before. He watched Beth grow up and grew considerably himself. She thought of him as her man of the desert and believed she understood his hard life, wild ways and quickness to fight—yet always gentle and thoughtful toward her.

Beth remembered the sad day her grandfather ordered John Skinner off the ranch when he had come with the stated intention to court her. He had been nearly thirty and she barely fifteen, and to the man who loved his granddaughter, that was an outrage. The old man had been angry for days at what he considered to be a betrayal of his trust in making his young namesake welcome at the ranch.

The morning passed slowly for Beth and grew even hotter. Noontime found them skirting along the toe of a tall butte. They came upon an acre or so of extra large junipers and French called a halt in their midst.

He untied his canteen and, stalking over to Beth, offered it to her. It was the first time anyone had offered her water since they had left camp at daybreak and she was extremely thirsty. As she reached for it, French grabbed her hand with his free one and held the soft woman flesh. His eyes pierced deeply into hers, relishing the flawless blue, and he felt the smoothness of her skin against the rough callousness of his palm and fingers.

She jerked free and he grinned. As she tilted the canteen and drank, he lay down full length in the shade and rested, scrutinizing her every move.

Her nearness and the faint odor of her femaleness excited him. His pulse increased and his arms ached to enclose, hug, and squeeze her. For a moment the desire to have her blanked out the presence of the watching men.

Beth sensed his overwhelming passion and her own lack of defense. For the first time in her life she was terribly afraid of a man. She got up and quickly moved out into the hot sunlight. Quietly she shivered.

A low, coarse guffaw of one of the men reached her.

The big black stallion was heavily scarred on neck and withers and the top of his left ear was missing. It had disappeared into the vicious mouth of the giant roan during the fight when the dark one had stolen the roan's harem of mares. Those nineteen contented females, their round, glossy rumps glistening in the afternoon sun, grazed the golden grass on the hillside below his lookout. From time to time they would look up and check the safety of their colts and prick their ears toward the stud, listening for any signal from him.

The large, black eyes in the intelligent head of the stallion saw everything that moved in his domain. From his elevation he saw the rolling hills dropping away slowly to the east and the desert, and to the west the land rising more steeply, climbing to the ridge. Beyond the skyline he knew the land plunged suddenly into a deep valley.

A young male, one of last year's colts still hanging on to the edge of the band, bothered the stallion. Except for him, the stallion had driven off all the other young studs soon after the

new colts had been born. The young males, alone and on
their own for the first time, ganged up in bachelor groups.
They now roamed from water hole to water hole and from
one good grazing area to another that might be even better,
making long, winding treks across the land. By the time the
strongest of them had accumulated his own harem, he would
know every hill, valley, and watering place for many miles in
all directions.

But this one yearling stud had not departed and for some
unaccountable reason still tried to follow his dam. At times
he would sidle up close to her and stretch out his neck as a
sign he would like a suck at her full udder. She would nip at
him and walk away, this year's colt, all legs, tripping along
close beside her and carefully watching the intruder.

Climbing up off the flat land in the early morning hours,
Peter Pipe had continued straight west into the rolling hills.
There was no sign of man, either white or Indian, or cattle as
he worked his way upward from one series of ridges to the
next higher one. He had ridden the sinks, eroded washes, and
very lowest passes between the hills to offer the least possible
opportunity for his pursuers to skyline and discover him.

The alert black stallion and Peter spotted each other at the
very same moment as Peter rode up out of a low draw, about
a quarter mile separating them. The stud stamped his front
feet excitedly on the stony ground and whirled in a short,
tight circle on top of his lookout.

He spooked down the hill, bugling a loud commanding
whinny out across the grass and sagebrush. The mares instantly came to attention. Sweeping across the rear of the
band, he nipped and crowded them in the direction he had
selected for escape. Sensing quickly the intention of the
master, the lead mare broke from the milling herd and raced
away, the others immediately following.

Like a great black dog herding sheep, the stallion rushed

back and forth urging the stragglers to hurry. Then when satisfied all were accounted for, he raced straight through the group. He sidestepped to miss the colts, but as he hurried past the yearling male, he bit him savagely on the rump, tearing out a chunk of skin half as big as a man's hand.

He passed the pilot mare and took up position about three lengths in front. None of the others had seen or heard the danger, but in strict obedience fought to keep up. The excited little colts, their lungs pumping hard and ungainly, long legs threatening to get out of control, fought to maintain station on their mothers.

Peter stopped and in pleasured awe watched the drove of wild horses flow along, their long, unpruned tails streaming out and whipping the tops of the brush. They raced straight away, climbing steadily until they vanished behind a shoulder of the mountain.

Good-looking animals, he decided, and thought of Skinner and his herd. None of this band would have to be killed because they were ugly and not quality.

At the crest of the topmost ridge, Peter climbed stiffly down and gazed into a wide, grass-covered valley. The land depicted on his map ended here. He had expected some dramatic change in the terrain to coincide with the edge of the map and this nearly vertical west-facing rampart of the mountain was surely that.

A symbol for water, a spring, marked the exact edge of the map. He figured the water hole must be just below him in one of the half-dozen small canyons. All of the canyons were very much alike, narrow, steep-walled, and cut the west-facing body of the mountain like the claw marks of a giant lion.

He rode along the mountainside just above where the canyons headed up and ended, looking for a sign to indicate the location of the water. And there it was, a foot-wide horse trail, and other smaller, winding game paths, leading down into one slit of a canyon. So well-worn were the trails, he knew they could only be heading toward water.

Peter followed the horse pathway, dropping rapidly down below the rims of the canyon. Heat from the slanting early afternoon sun had built up in the confined space between the rock walls and he began to sweat.

The water of the spring seeped up out of the dirt of the canyon bottom. Horses, deer, and other animals had waded and pawed the mud and drank from tiny puddles, most only footprints full of water. The animals defecated where they stood and created a dirty and unwholesome quagmire.

At the upper end of the bog, after much digging in the soft ooze, Peter found the source where the clean, fresh water bubbled forth. He let it wash clear and lay down and drank his fill. After replenishing his canteens, he allowed the thirsty horses to drink.

In a little under thirty hours, he had ridden over eighty miles of rough, inhospitable land, and he and the horses were exhausted. They must rest, but it was too hot to sleep in the canyon and he knew it was dangerous to stay near the water. He expected the posse to come down from above following his trail, so he led his mounts a mile or so down the gulch. As he approached the mouth of the canyon opening out into the valley, the heat lessened and he selected a small hillock above the hot floor and there found a pleasant, gentle breeze blowing.

He loosened the cinches on the horses, tied rope hobbles to the front legs of the gray, who had the greatest tendency to stray off, pulled a coarse, woollen blanket from the pack, and lay down in the grass and went immediately to sleep.

CHAPTER 9

Groggy and half asleep, Peter awoke to the bawling of thirsty cattle. He raised his head and shading the low angle rays of the setting sun from his eyes with his hand, looked around. His horses stood close by looking intently down the canyon. Turning his eyes in that direction, he saw a herd of about thirty cows pushed by two riders just entering the canyon.

One of the riders spotted Peter's saddle horses.

"Watch it, Sam, saddle horses ahead," he said quickly and yanked his rifle from its scabbard beneath his leg.

The other immediately did the same.

They had not yet seen Peter, but he was caught in the open and knew if they came a few steps closer they would discover him. He rose up out of the foot-tall grass, bareheaded and crestfallen, angry at himself for being so easily caught. But surely they could not know he had robbed a bank and was wanted by the law.

"Hello," he called out to the horsemen some thirty-five or forty yards away. He let his right hand fall from shading his eyes from the bright sun to near the butt of his pistol and raised the left to shield his eyes.

The two men saw him the instant he stood up and quickly swung their rifles to cover him. One was middle-aged and the second about ten years younger. Both wore dirty clothes that had not seen a washtub for a considerable time, and their mahogany faces, burned by long days in the sun and wind, had several days' growth of beard. Their ferret eyes watched Peter with intense suspicion.

Peter did not trust the looks of the two. He glanced at the cows and quickly counted three different brands. The men must be rustlers, hunting a hidden water hole where they could change the brands and wait for the burns to heal.

"Stay right there, my sleepy friend, and don't make any sudden moves," ordered the older man. Without taking his eyes off Peter, he spoke to the other man. "Sam, ride up on that point a ways and look up to the head of the gulch and see if there's anyone else with him."

The one called Sam spurred his horse up the slope, checked along the canyon, and hurried back down. "Nope, no one there, Les. He's alone."

"Where are you from?" queried Les.

"Westfall."

"And why are you on this side of the Alvord with a packhorse?"

"Had a falling out with some people."

"Who?"

"Sheriff, among others," answered Peter, hoping he was guessing correctly, that the two were outlaws.

"Well, well, and why do you tell us that? Ain't you afraid we might turn you over to Gumert?" grinned Les. The rifle stayed riveted onto Peter's chest.

Peter did not answer.

"Sam, check his gear and see what he has we can use," ordered Les.

"Good-looking horses at least," said Sam, as he rode past Peter, "and a fair-size pack of supplies."

"Yeh, I can see that too. We sure can stand some better

horses for a change after those crow-bait nags we have been riding."

Peter measured the man, resting easy on his mount more than one hundred feet away. A difficult target for a six-gun after a quick draw. At this range the rifle Les held so comfortably midway between his lap and shoulder would be deadly.

The piercing rays of the setting sun streaming in just above and to the left of Les forced Peter to squint heavily. He stepped left to lessen the directness of the rays into his eyes and get a clearer view of the sun.

The movement was not lost on Les and he shifted the barrel of the gun to keep it trained on Peter. "Now, young fellow, I know the sun might be bothering you, but that is the way I want it. So just stay put right there." He licked his lips and grinned.

Out of the corner of his eye Peter saw Sam approaching the roan and the saddlebags. Once they found the gold and paper money, he knew he was as good as dead.

"Good God, Les, it's full of money!" exclaimed Sam in a high, excited voice as he untied the saddlebag.

For one unguarded second, Les turned his head slightly and shifted his eyes to his partner.

Peter drew and fired. It was a long shot, maybe too long. But then the man flinched at the punch of the bullet. It ripped the skin and flesh and skittered along the outside of the ribbed cage of his chest.

The rifle came up to the man's aiming eye with amazing swiftness and cracked harshly.

Something slapped Peter's upper left arm. He aimed the six-gun, now lifted to eye level, and squeezed off another shot, straight and true. Though pierced through the heart, Les still sat his saddle for a fraction of a second, then tumbled sideways to the stony ground.

Fear at that wasted piece of a second he had waited for Les

to fall almost panicked Peter. He knew he should have already been firing on the second man. The barrel of his pistol
whirled right to find Sam's gun lining up on him. Peter continued his turn into a fall to the right. Before he hit the
ground, the pistol bucked in his hand as he shot Sam through
the chest.

The smashing chunk of lead hurled the man backward into
the roan horse, which lunged away. The unsupported body of
the man hit the ground, flopped onto its face, and lay quiet.

All of Peter's attention had been focused on getting the
shot off accurately and he had fallen heavily onto some rocks.
He lay there bruised, recovering his wind, and was surprised
when his left arm began to pain and throb, for he had fallen
onto his right side.

He felt the place on his arm that hurt and his hand came
away from the sleeve wet with blood. There was a rip in the
cloth and he tore it more open and explored the flesh inside.
The rounded outer muscle of his arm had a groove-shaped
wound where the bullet had plowed through, big enough
for him to lay a finger in it.

Taking his bandana from around his neck, he fashioned a
crude tourniquet above the gaping wound. He twisted it tight
with a short length of stick until the bright blood stopped
flowing and tucked the end of the piece of wood under the
cloth so it would not come loose. From a strip of his shirttail,
he made a crude bandage and tied up the wound.

After tying the saddlebag on the roan shut so the money
would not fall out, he whistled for the gray horse. He came
part way back from where he had spooked during the shooting, but shied away from the bodies and odor of death.

Suddenly Peter felt quite weak and there was a slight trem-
ble in his hands and legs. He dropped down on the blanket
and held his knees with his hands, but the jerking continued.

"Damn!" Peter exclaimed, willing his body to regain control from the reaction to the wound and violence.

As the trembling subsided, he realized he had not yet reloaded. Shaking his head at the dangerous lapse of safety, he ejected the empty shell casings and inserted fresh cartridges. After he finished, he looked west, but nothing moved out on the valley. He turned and searched back up the mountain in the direction from which he had come. But no living thing stirred there either. He was alone with two dead men in an endless land of mountains and valleys.

Peter did not go near the corpses as he unsaddled their two jaded horses and let them drift off up the canyon with the cattle. Then for a long time he studied the map and looked west across the valley toward unknown land. He could see at least twenty miles, to where the hills began to build up again on the opposite side of the low country. But that land did not show on the map, and even though he saw it was little different from what he had crossed, he could not force himself to venture from the map. He was not yet ready for that long, lonely journey into an unnamed land.

Gently he rolled up the deerskin map and carefully fitted it back inside his shirt. Folding up the blanket, he walked down between the bodies and shoved it into the packsaddle. In the gathering dusk he rode due north along the edge of the land encompassed by the map.

"All right if I build a fire to warm up some grub for you?" asked Perrine.

"Yeah, there is nobody within twenty miles of us," answered French. "But use only dry wood and build it back between those big rocks." He pointed to two large boulders about shoulder tall at the base of the rimrock.

"That's the only kind there is," responded Perrine. "The

drought has been so bad even green wood burns with almost no smoke." He busied himself with the fire.

The lava rimrock, with a few stunted junipers visible along the top, threw the whole party into shadow. Shorty relaxed in the welcome shade and watched the sparks from the fire rise straight up in the windless evening.

Perrine had rendezvoused with the fleeing gang this evening of the second day as Shorty and Storms had the first day. And this camp was dry as had been the other one, deliberately selected by him without water so any pursuer would have a thirsty, hard time of it. And the strategy was working, there was absolutely no sign of pursuit.

Shorty glanced at Beth sitting slumped against the base of a large rock. He caught her watching him and she smiled wanly, her eyes tired and the tip of her nose badly sunburned. Quickly he looked away, for he wanted to develop no feeling or attachment for her, but he could not help thinking the sunburn must be painful. But she had not complained once during the hard ride covering nearly one hundred miles in two days.

Shorty watched Perrine examine Beth, his eyes undressing her. Though she was dusty and disheveled, her beautiful face, rounded hips, and full bosom drew French's stare again and again. She lowered her head and looked at the ground.

The other three men were silent and gave no apparent attention to the girl, but Shorty sensed French's deep attraction for her. To his knowledge, none of them had really bothered her—yet. Once in a permanent camp and the men rested, her problems would begin.

"It's ready," called Perrine. "While you eat, I'll take the horses over the ridge of the hills," and he pointed to the west, "and turn them loose."

French nodded without speaking.

"Do you have enough water to give them a drink before you turn them loose?" asked Shorty.

"Nope. Just enough for us and the horses we will be riding," answered Perrine.

"Too bad," said Shorty. "There's no water within several miles around here and they won't get that far even if they knew which direction to go. They're as good as dead."

"Can't help that," said Perrine, and he walked off toward the horses tied to the sagebrush.

Perrine rode out leading the animals through the falling darkness. As the thin crescent of the moon sailed up above the horizon, the five weary riders sat balancing tin plates on their knees and silently ate.

Shorty unrolled his blanket on the ground, still warm with memories of the heat of the day. He made himself comfortable, facing upward toward the sky.

Weaker and weaker stars came to life as the darkness deepened, and soon the sky was full of tiny pricks of light. Then a series of the twinkling lights were blotted out by the bulk of the rising moon, only for them to be born again as the heavenly body continued upward and uncovered them. In the blackness he heard Perrine return and stake out the remaining horses on the ends of lariats.

Much later during the night he heard movement and from its location thought it was Perrine again. The man walked away and soon returned leading the horses and tied them to a picket line near where the saddles had been tossed on the ground.

Shorty heard Perrine whispering off near where Beth had spread her blankets. Beth's voice said something in return. Shorty sat and cupped his hands around his ears to hear better and aimed them at the nighttime conversation.

". . . someone to protect you," whispered Perrine.

Shorty considered interfering, but could think of no gain

for himself. Then, against the lighter darkness of the starlit sky, French got up and slipped soundlessly upon the talkers. Shorty slid his six-gun from its holster, raised to a crouched position, and moved forward half the distance to Beth.

Boots scuffled and stomped the hard ground, and the blinking stars were snuffed out with quick movement as two men strained with labored breath against each other. French broke free and his hard fist smacked on the bare flesh of the side of Perrine's head and almost instantly another blow to the nose, knocking him to the ground with a thump.

Perrine lay moaning. "You broke my nose. I'm bleeding bad."

No one paid him any attention. Shorty watched the faint outline of French return and kneel beside Beth.

"Don't do that. Keep your hands off me."

"Hold still, I won't hurt you."

A subdued and muted struggle drifted to Shorty as French fondled Beth. Shorty knew he should not be where he was—this was French's business. But instead of retreating, his thumb cocked the six-gun.

"Leave me alone. Please! You're hurting me."

"Hold still, I tell you, or I'll slap you."

Shorty squatted down low. "Is she hurt?" he called out in the darkness.

Complete silence held for a handful of seconds. French stood up and Shorty saw his silhouette from the waist up against the sky. His hand was thrust outward and Shorty knew he held a pistol.

"That you, Shorty?" French's head turned from side to side, trying to locate him in the blackness.

Shorty let additional seconds drag past. For a moment he felt a strong urge to shoot French, grab the girl, and ride back to Westfall. It would be easy to blast a slug through the outline of the man.

"Shorty, I want you to take care of the girl. See that no one bothers her."

"All right," answered Shorty, but he did not stand up.

He could see French still trying to spot him in the darkness. Then the man holstered his gun and walked off in the gloom.

Shorty stole silently to the girl's side. "You all right, miss?"

"Yes, and thank you very much for helping me."

He did not answer; instead he knelt down and felt around on the ground with his hands until he found what he wanted.

"Here, take these two rocks and keep them handy. Throw them at me if you need my help again. Now, try to hit me if you can, so I'll be sure to hear them hit the ground. Do you know where my blankets are?"

"Yes. But I would rather have a pistol or your knife."

"You know I can't give you either one of those things. Now, I would much rather you throw the rocks than call out to me. It would be best for both of us if no one knew I was coming to help you. Do you understand?"

"Yes, I will do as you ask."

"Then don't worry so much. I'll be just over there. Rest now and go to sleep. We will be on our way again in a little while." He felt her hand softly touch his chest, as if telling him she trusted him, and then it was quickly removed. As he slipped away in the blackness, he wished she had not touched him. His one brief moment of weakness when he came to her aid and her contact with him did not establish a pact between them. He knew he was not to be trusted.

CHAPTER 10

Tense and wary, Skinner's eyes searched the broken rimrock cutting across the trail a long rifle shot ahead. Through the shimmering heat waves, he detected no movement of man or animals. Even the birds and insects hid from the burning sun. But somewhere along the trail the kidnappers would ambush anyone following them and this just might be the place.

Skinner paid special attention to the brush on the top of the rim, for that was the most likely place for one of the outlaws to lie in hiding and guard the kidnappers' back trail. From that high point the outlaw could spot Skinner from a long distance and keep him in view in the stunted junipers below. And in the event the outlaw's ambush failed, he could ride out and have a long head start before Skinner could find a trail up to the top of the rimrock and give chase.

Running his eyes in a zigzag pattern back and forth over the land, Skinner shortened the range of his investigation to right up under his own horse's hooves. The stallion stood on the dusty prints left by the outlaw gang.

This was the middle of the third day and Skinner had yet to see any sign of another human except horse tracks and the imprint of boots. The few thunderheads of the first day had dissipated quickly in the late afternoon. Once one of them had leaked a thin curtain of rain from a great height, but the moisture had been sucked back into the parched air before it could reach the ground. All tracks still lay as visible as when first made, and he followed them easily.

His first night camp had been dry. He had started with a gallon canteen of water for his own use, and four gallons for the horses. With that forty-plus pounds of water, he estimated a travel range of one hundred miles. When he found the outlaws' first camp and discovered it was dry and that they had cached water and a fresh relay of horses, he knew they might have done the same at subsequent camps and it would be a long and difficult trail.

Briefly leaving the pursuit, Skinner had followed a game trail hoping to find water. The horses badly needed ten to fifteen gallons apiece. But when the water was found, it proved to be only a tiny, slow seep and the thirsty horses sucked the two or three gallons dry in a few seconds. Skinner returned to the trail and again took up the chase.

A magpie flapped lazily from the base of the rimrock, climbed upward on black and white wings, and disappeared behind it. At no time had the alert bird showed any alarm, and Skinner, satisfied that this probably was not the place of ambush, nudged his horse forward with his heels. With luck the scavenger bird could have found and be giving away the site of the outlaw camp.

Slow and cautious, for even a magpie could sometimes be fooled, Skinner approached the takeoff point of the bird. About a hundred yards out, he pulled the tired stallion and mare up and surveyed for several minutes what appeared to be the kidnappers' last camp. Nothing stirred, so he slowly entered, his rifle at the ready.

He stepped down from the saddle. While his thirsty animals rested, he minutely examined the camp. He saw where they had cooked, slept, and had the picket line tied. Then he found the black, crusted patch of blood in the dirt and quickly knelt down beside it. But only the large boot prints of a man were near it and he sighed softly in relief. Fervently he hoped that any blood he ever found belonged to someone other than Beth.

On foot, he circled the camp looking for water. He detected tracks where someone had led off the tired horses and returned alone and a much older sign that had been made when the camp was set up, but that was all. There was no surface water and no green vegetation that might indicate the presence of groundwater at a shallow depth. The gang's escape route had been planned by someone well acquainted with the land.

For two days Skinner had pressed rapidly, and at times recklessly, along the trail. Even after his quarry had acquired fresh horses, he had fallen behind only five or six hours. But all that was now changed. His horses had had only three gallons of water apiece in over two days and within the next day must be provided a full and satisfying drink, even if that meant abandoning the pursuit entirely. Skinner had drunk the last of his water ration the evening before and had only his body moisture to survive on until more was found. And strange, unknown country did not easily supply water in a drought.

He returned to the camp and stood in the shade. Though he had eaten little since taking the trail and was slightly hungry now, that was all right for he had brought only a small amount of food, having kept the load light to travel faster. But now he was at the point he must survive at the expense of the horses if necessary.

He walked over to the mare and took a tin cup from the pack. Squatting down beside her, he pressed his head in tight against her stomach just in front of her rear leg and began to squeeze and pull, firmly yet gently, on the stubby teats extending from the short, sacklike udder.

Skinner milked a full cup of the rich, creamy liquid. But it had taken every drop the mare had, for in her dehydrated condition she was drying up and would give no more milk until properly and amply watered.

After sitting down in the shade of the rock near where the gang had built their fire, Skinner put the cup to his lips and sipped the warm, tasty liquid. A horsehair, floating along with the fluid inside his mouth, tickled his tongue. He isolated it in the side of his mouth, swallowed the milk, and then fished the hair out and flicked it onto the ground. He sat contemplating the mare as he finished the drink. His plan to use her milk as food and as a source of good water, in the event potable water was not found for him but less pure water was found for the horses, was not working out.

Well, since I don't know where a water hole is, I may as well tag along the tracks until I find a well-worn game path to follow, thought Skinner. He mounted the stallion and again started along the trail that was gradually growing old and would soon be cold.

Peter Pipe slept fitfully rolled up in his blanket. He had ridden until it was too dark to travel and had made a dry camp on a small flat about halfway up the upthrust side of the fault-block mountain.

Though the arm had stopped bleeding and he had removed the tourniquet, the bullet wound throbbed with pain and he could not rest comfortably. The crude bandage was a mass of dry, crusted blood and stuck in the raw flesh of the wound.

At the first light of morning he was up. He cut a strip from one of the blankets and made a sling, hung it around his neck, and rested his sore arm in it.

He had a difficult time doing his chores, especially saddling the horses. At first he could not get the cinch tight, afraid he would start bleeding again, but finally he got the leather strap up through the metal ring and the hitch pulled somewhat tight. He decided it was good enough to keep the saddle from turning under the horse's belly and end up dumping him on the ground. He rode away from camp following a well-beaten game trail that hung onto the contour of the mountain.

The dawn came to life, the high thin clouds of the morning, a silent explosion of red and orange fanning out across the eastern sky. The first rays of the early September sun slanted down warm and pleasant—unusually warm—giving no hint of the frigid wind and heavy snow that would freeze and smother the high desert country in a couple of months.

The trail led Peter through patches of bitterbrush, the favorite food of deer, and scattered junipers growing on the topmost reaches of the mountain, existing there thanks to the increased snow and rain squeezed out of the clouds by the forced lifting of the air to cross the higher rims. Grass and sagebrush clothed the lower slopes and valley bottom, and along the dry stream channels a sprinkling of willows sank long roots deep under the dusty surface gravels, searching for life-sustaining water.

Peter was not hungry, but he forced a little dried fruit down as he rode along developing his strategy. Originally he had planned to travel straight away from Westfall, ride right out of the country with the $8,000. But since he was now not going to do that, he had a more difficult task—to hide his trail and lose the posse.

Every stretch of hard ground and rocky area was used to cover his tracks. Often he would turn in the center of such an area and take a completely new direction. But usually he rode straight across so that he was not predictable. Having no place in particular to arrive at and no particular time to get there in, he wandered at random.

In midmorning the winding game trails he had been seeing

began to straighten out and come together. Water must not be far off, he figured.

An hour later, after continually taking the more used trails, he found the spring dripping down from under a ledge of rock tall enough for him to ride up under. It was cool in the shade of the rock. He dismounted gingerly, favoring his arm. While the horses drank, he checked his location on the map and found a symbol for a spring he believed was this one.

After an hour's rest he headed east, winding around and up and down through what seemed an endless number of small rolling hills. About noon he topped out on a ridge and looked down across a wide flat.

Not more than a quarter mile distant six riders, one of them leading an extra horse, crossed the trail ahead, riding at a trot to the north. Quickly Peter backed his horses below the skyline and crouched down, peering through the grass of the hilltop to watch the strange horsemen.

It could not possibly be the posse, he reasoned. That had to be behind him, somewhere to the west, assuming the sheriff still trailed him. And from what Skinner had told him about the lawman, he would not give up easily.

In a few minutes the group of riders dropped into a low spot and he did not see them again. He sat for a while longer figuring the different possibilities the presence of the strangers meant.

Finally, he shrugged his shoulders, forgetting his wound for a moment, and winced at the stab of pain. If the sheriff was dogging his trail, as he was sure the man was, then what better place to hide hoofprints than in the sign of the six horsemen? However, he would head south, backtracking along the route the riders had come.

He had anticipated a straight, direct route, but instead from time to time the riders had changed direction, often when least expected. Also, they did as he had done, ride the

hard ground and dense stands of brush in which they meandered. And then for no apparent reason, they would
straighten their course and hurry away at a lope or trot.

As he worked the trail south, it picked up a dry stream bed
and followed along it. The hills gradually crowded in until
the stream was squeezed into a steep-walled canyon a hundred yards or so wide. The trail followed along a bench on the
right side, thrusting through dense sagebrush, belly high to
the horses.

A long time before, there had been a rock slide from above,
and the jumble of fallen blocks extended out onto the bench,
crowding the path to the very brink of the wash, lying ten
feet or so below a steep, eroded cutbank. Peter rode cautiously, watching the trail but letting the horses pick their
own way. Carefully, they sidled past the narrowest spot and
turned safely away from the crumbly bank.

The man and horses were suddenly there, not fifty yards
away, heading up the creek toward Peter. Each saw the other
at the same moment. The man was fast, a rifle suddenly ap-
pearing in his hand. Peter kicked free of the stirrups and tumbled to the right. He drew his pistol quickly and squatted,
concealed for the moment in the brush.

Had the man also jumped from his horse? Peter thought
so, but everything had happened so fast, all he was sure of
was there had been a rider with a rifle. Peter's horses stood,
ears pointing down the trail. A soft, questioning nicker from
the man's horse drifted up the wash. The animals did not yet
know the deadly intent of the men.

Peter's arm ached and fresh blood oozed through the bandage. He remembered the dangerous episode of the rustlers'
catching him in the open through his own mistake. And he
knew he had better move, change locations fast so the man
could not trap him. But where to move? The other man had
the advantage of a wide piece of the bench and the brush

growing part way up the hillside, while Peter was caught against the rock fall, the steep open slope, and the wash. He would have to go down into the dry channel.

Cautiously, bent far over, he crabbed sideways to the brink of the wash, sat down, holstered his gun, and slid himself over. He used both hands, and the sharp stab of pain from his wounded arm made him catch his breath. But he managed to lower himself to the bottom without rolling a rock or raising dust. He pulled the six-gun out and wished he had a rifle, for there could be some long-range shooting. As silently as a snake, he slithered along, pressed close to the nearly vertical, protective bank.

A hundred feet downstream he raised his head up an inch to look. The man's horses stood a few feet away watching Peter's animals, apparently unaware of his nearness.

"Hey, you," called the man, "I've got you boxed in. If your name is Peter, you had better sing out."

Peter's heart jumped at the sudden sound of the human voice reverberating in the narrow canyon. The man was over near where he had been and surely did not have him boxed in, but he did have the high ground on him. The voice sounded somewhat familiar, but distorted as it was by the rough, confined walls of the canyon, Peter was not sure whose it was.

"Is that you, Skinner?" he yelled up the hill toward the source of the voice.

"Yeh, this is Skinner."

"Are you with the posse after me?"

"Hell no, Peter. You know I wouldn't be trailing you. I'm after a bunch of kidnapping bastards that rode off with Beth Manderfield."

"Can we talk?" asked Peter.

"Sure enough."

"I'm standing up then," and Peter slowly poked his head above the sagebrush.

The red-headed man stood up, a sheepish grin on his freckled face. He had climbed the side of the hills silently, had been looking down to where he had thought Peter was hunkered in the brush, and was surprised when the young man emerged into the open, close to his horses.

"Peter, you are pretty good with a pistol, and it seems you are learning a few other tricks, too." Holding his rifle chest high, he waded down through the sagebrush to Peter.

"I had a hard lesson yesterday and didn't want another today. How did you know it was me?"

"Recognized your gray horse after I climbed high enough to see him good. Now let's get out of this narrow place because it's not safe in here," said Skinner, swinging up on his horse.

Peter hurried up the dead watercourse to his animals. Skinner rode along behind.

"Which way?" asked Peter, mounting.

"Up the wash. I've got a lot of distance to make up."

They back tracked along Peter's trail and came out into the open valley.

"What did you mean, someone had kidnapped Beth?" asked Peter when they pulled up and stopped.

"A couple of Mexicans rode into Manderfield's place, shot and killed Miguel, and rode off with the girl. Demanded seventy-five thousand dollars to be delivered in a few days. Are you riding with me after them?"

"You know I am. Are you sure they are out this way?"

Skinner shook his head. "Damn, I'm not about to make a mistake about that. This is the third day I've been after them. They had water and fresh horses staked out and that's why I lost some ground."

"About noon, six riders cut across in front of me, heading

north," said Peter. "I wasn't sure if they were Indians or white men. I was using their tracks to hide my own sign. Since I followed them right back to you, they must be the ones you were tracking."

"That's good. They're not as far ahead as I thought, and they couldn't have been Indians since all of them are held on the reservation by the Army, or so they say. How much water you got? I'm plumb dried up."

"Two gallons or a little less, but I know where there is a spring with good water."

"How far off this trail?"

"Must be eight or ten miles."

"Damn, I wished there was water closer than that, but I can't go any longer without watering down real well."

Peter pulled the map from his shirt. "My dad made me a map covering this land and he did a good job. Let's just see where he shows the next water to be to the north."

Skinner reined his horse in beside Peter and reached out and helped him hold the map. "Looks like you're bleeding some," he observed.

"Yes, but not too bad. I believe it'll quit in a little while."

"We'll doctor it when we stop tonight and you can tell me about it," said Skinner.

"All right, but look here. The map shows there is water in the bottom of a big valley about one day's ride north. Do you think the gang that has Beth is going that direction?"

"They had me fooled at first, but now I have it figured out. They are circling the Alvord. Now, see over there?" Skinner pointed. "Westfall, where they started. Then they rode around the south end of the Alvord, keeping well back in the hills, then gradually turned west and now north. The way I got it calculated is they are heading for the Honeycombs Badlands. Then when they go for the ransom, they just ride hard and fast to the south for five or six hours and they can

be back at Westfall. But now they have more riding to the
north to do and will pass through that valley. If it's the one I
think it is, it is called Mormon Valley."

"So, what about the water?"

"Let's take a drink ourselves and give the rest to my horses,
since they have been dry for two days except for a little alkali
water last evening, and ride straight north."

"And if the water isn't there? My map doesn't show any
other water for thirty miles or so."

"It had better be there."

They each took a long pull from the canteens. Skinner
poured what was left in one canteen into his hat and held it
out for the stallion. He slurped it up with three or four powerful swigs. The mare extended her graceful neck and sniffed
the hat as the horse drank.

Skinner refilled the hat with the last water from the second
canteen. Wanting to drink that, too, the stallion crowded in
close and Skinner kicked him away so the mare could get her
share.

"That's only a drop to them. Looks like it's going to be a
long, dry spell," said Skinner, draining the last few drops from
both canteens into his mouth. "Let's move out," he said as he
climbed astride the big stallion.

CHAPTER 11

"You're turning back? What in the hell for?" rasped Sheriff Gumert. He was hot and tired and in no mood to be polite to the three riders bunched up before him.

"Sheriff, we have been on this Pipe kid's trail for nearly three days and it's getting older and we're falling farther behind all the time," answered the roustabout from the feedstore.

"You've got a tender ass, that's your problem," snapped the sheriff. "You should've stayed in town and toted those sacks of feed around." He turned to the other two posse members who wanted to quit. "And what are your reasons? Can't you go without a beer for longer than three days, or are you a little shy about coming up against the Pipe fellow after he killed those two riders with the cattle?"

"Now, Sheriff, that ain't no way to talk to us, and that ain't the reason we're turning back. I didn't have any money in the bank like Jake and maybe some of you others, so I don't stand to gain anything from catching the fellow."

"How about just being a good citizen? Oh, hell, that don't mean anything to any of you three. Get the hell out of here and I hope you get lost," said the sheriff in disgust.

The men turned their horses and headed along the back

trail. Ignoring them, the sheriff eyed the remaining riders of the posse.

"I appreciate you men sticking with me. We'll catch this gent even though he does seem to know the country real well."

The sheriff examined the dark, sunburned faces of the Fettus brothers. He couldn't figure why they hadn't headed back with the others. But them, they often did things that were hard to understand.

"Let's move out," he said.

An hour later, following Peter's trail, they found the spring under the rock ledge.

"We'll take a few minutes' break while we water the horses and fill the canteens," said the sheriff, climbing down. "Ollie, come over here and talk with me and let one of your brothers take care of your horse," he directed.

The sheriff seated himself on a rock in the shade at the far end of the ledge. Ollie sidled up and squatted down beside him, his eyes alert but hooded with half-closed eyelids.

"Ollie, I've heard you've ridden this country over here on this side of the Alvord. Now, let's consider a situation where you had robbed a bank and killed two men you ran into while trying to escape. Now those men may have been rustlers, but that doesn't make any difference for what we're talking about."

Ollie shook his head and started to say something.

The sheriff continued, "I realize you would never do any of these things and have the law after you. But just for the sake of talking, let's assume you did. Now, starting from right here and not leaving this part of the country, what would you do?"

Ollie's furtive animal eyes flitted across Gumert's face and then came to rest, looking intently out to the northeast. How badly did he want to kill that smart-aleck kid? Was it enough to tell about the spring in the badlands? He had always reserved that spot for a time when he might desperately need a hideout. His mind made up, he turned to the sheriff.

"Over that way, far back in the Honeycombs there's a spring—really two springs, a fair-sized one and a much littler one down the draw from the first. It's about two days' ride from here. Very few people know about it and it's easy to post a lookout and spot anyone coming. That's where I would go."

The sheriff nodded. "Sounds good. Any other water holes in that direction?"

"I'm not certain, but I've seen a few deer and wild mustangs pretty far out from that water so there might be. I just don't know of any in particular."

The sheriff stood up and paced back to the others. "Make sure your horses drink their fill and you, too. We're leaving the trail and striking straight out for the badlands where this bank-robbing jasper just might be heading."

"And if he's not there?" asked Jake. "What then?"

"We'll swing back to the south in a long circle until we pick up the sign again, that's what. Now fill the canteens level full."

They made camp in the dusk of the evening with no water for either man or horses. Skinner's mounts were in distress from lack of water and restlessly stomped about in their hobbles. The two belonging to Peter wandered around nibbling at the dry, stiff grass, nearly all of it carry-over stems from the previous year.

"I sure don't like to treat animals that way," said Skinner, nodding toward his mounts.

"Me either," agreed Peter. "They deserve to be fed and watered right."

"Let me look at that wound," said Skinner. He rummaged

in the bottom of his pack, found a small tin of Rosebud Salve, and sat down near Peter. "How did this happen?"

Peter, flinching from time to time as Skinner worked the bandage loose from the bullet wound, told of the encounter with the rustlers.

"This salve heals the horses when they get hurt and did the same for me, too, a couple of times when I got cut, so I guess it will heal you, too."

Skinner pried the lid from the flat tin of salve, dipped his finger into the amber, jellied ointment, and spread a blob of it generously on the gaping, red flesh.

"We were lucky in getting that bandage loose with only a little bleeding. With this oily medicine on it, the next one won't stick so much." Skinner pressed the lid of the Rosebud tin into place and stowed it away again in his pack.

Under a completely dark moon, a pitch-black night settled over the desert. Skinner and Peter sat on their spread blankets, near enough to talk to each other in low voices. But they were silent for awhile, each staring off into the gloom. The soft thud of hooves as the horses moved and the swish and rustle of the grass drifted to them on the slow, warm wind.

"The gang that took Beth, what will they do to her?" asked Peter in a low voice.

Skinner did not answer for a moment, then his voice came out flat and emotionless. "The same thing all men do to pretty women when they have them in their power."

"What do you mean?"

"They will breed her like a stud does a mare."

"All of them?"

"Maybe, maybe not, could be the leader is strong enough to keep her for himself. If he isn't, all the men will have a go at her." Peter was silent, and Skinner could only dimly make out his form. "Does that change your feelings toward her?"

"I—I don't know. But I do know I'm going to kill them all,

every damn one of them." Peter's voice was ice in the blackness. He rubbed his calloused thumb along the smooth steel of the pistol barrel.

"*We* will kill them all, every damn one of them!" corrected Skinner, his own voice breaking and coming out hard with emotion.

Peter, his eyes moist and throat tight, could not trust himself to speak further. He was glad it was dark so Skinner could not see his face. The flurry of events whipping out of control around him scared him. Never had he been so enmeshed in the actions of others.

Finally Peter asked in a haunted voice, "Please tell me the whole story. Am I responsible? Did it happen because the sheriff was out of town after me?"

"Maybe some your fault. But I suspect they would have taken Beth sooner or later with Gumert right in his office." Then Skinner told Peter what he knew of Beth's abduction.

Skinner added, "Do you realize part of the money you stole from the bank belongs to Beth and Manderfield? And there is no guarantee they will get the money they had deposited, though I doubt that eight thousand dollars will ruin the bank."

"Mr. Manderfield said I misunderstood what my dad said when he told me to rob a bank if I needed money. I think he is correct and that I should give the money back. But how can I do that without going to prison?"

"I don't know. We may not come out of this alive and won't have to worry about it. But if we do make it, John Manderfield will have to take the lead to get you off."

"What do you expect the gang's next move to be?" asked Peter.

"First off, they don't want to be tracked into their hideout. That is their main worry regardless how well the trail is hid. So I would say they will set up an ambush for anyone trailing them. The problem for us is we don't know where and can't scout every likely place before we ride through. Even if we are right and they are laying in wait for us, they have a good chance of getting one or both of us."

Peter did not answer. He lay down, pulled the blanket up over himself, settled his sore arm as comfortably as possible, and rested. The stars wheeled slowly across the black-velvet heavens, and Peter watched them and wondered what the morrow would bring. He heard Skinner lie down and soon his dry, raspy breathing. The man was in nearly as bad condition as his horses, having had only one small drink of water in a day and a half.

CHAPTER 12

Pawonto, the Paiute warrior, and his son slipped stealthily upon the small band of deer—a buck, a few does, and their half-grown fawns. The first sunlight of the day, lighting the broken, rocky flank of the mountain, bathed the gray pelts of the deer and turned them into pewter statues. And the wind, having just finished its night-long fall into the valley, lay quiet and resting and not yet ready to begin the sun-heated uphill breeze of the day.

The warrior looked back across the mountainside but could not see his squaw. However, he knew she was hidden there with the horse and his bow and arrows, waiting for his signal to come and help with the skinning of the deer. Good dependable woman, he thought.

He glanced at his son, nearly as tall as he and well-muscled, and smiled. Today was an important day for the family and especially for the boy, the culmination of a plan Pawonto had begun several years ago.

Pawonto had retreated to the mountain ten years before, in 1878 after the Umatilla chief had, in terrible treachery and at the urging of the white man, killed the Paiute chief, Egan. Without their leader the Paiute tribe was defeated in a battle shortly thereafter by the white man's army led by General Oliver Howard. After such a costly defeat there would never be another attempt to reconquer their land from the whites.

At the end of the battle, on the banks of the Columbia River, Pawonto had escaped, slipping away with his woman and baby into the desert. He made a vow he would never be forced back onto the reservation and be locked up there to starve, as they had for so many years.

After a long march deep into the desert, the family of three took refuge on an uninhabited mountain lying at the head of a lava-rimmed valley. One small spring, high on the side of the brush- and juniper-covered mountain was the only permanent water for many miles in any direction.

Life had been calm and peaceful for them. Only once had he seen a white man and that was when a lost Mormon family had died of thirst in the bottom of the valley. Pawonto had happened upon them too late to help and left them as he had found them. Other white men came and buried the bodies. But by then, Pawonto and his family were hidden high on the mountain.

Pawonto grew concerned about his son as the years passed and when none of their people joined them. It was not good for the boy to grow to manhood without the association of others of his age, and the fights, contests, and lovemaking that went with it. So, Pawonto, as an example to the boy, revived the ancient custom of his people of proving manhood by running a mature male deer to exhaustion and then slaying it for food and its skin. At the end of the chase he would tell the growing boy that when he could also run a big buck down, he would be a man. Today was the day the boy would make his attempt.

The chase across the rough, brushy country would be long and grueling. The boy wore the lightest of clothing—a headband, tough moccasins, leggings to the knees, and a soft leather strap which tied his privates comfortably and firmly to his crotch. A sharp, steel knife was strapped to his waist. As by the old practice, it would be used to make the kill.

They were close to the deer. One of the does stopped walking, sniffed in, and sorted through the myriad of scents in the calm air with her supersensitive nose. Detecting nothing threatening, she relaxed and trotted a few paces to catch up with the others.

"Look him over very closely," whispered Pawonto, "so you will know him even if he mixes with a herd of other deer. Soon as he begins to run, carefully measure the size and shape of his hooves so that you know them among many tracks."

The son nodded. He had already been given the same instructions several times. And he was fifteen years old and had to be told only once.

He examined the stag in minute detail—gray with the smallest tinge of brown in his coat, three antler points on one side and four on the other, and one tine bent unnaturally inward until it almost touched the main beam.

"The right antler—see, it is different. And see the scar on the right rump," whispered Pawonto.

The boy nodded; he had missed the scar.

"Don't crowd him too hard or he will leave the valley," cautioned the man.

Now only twenty-five yards separated deer and men. The buck halted and froze into position, flicking his ears directly at the brush hiding the two humans. His moist, black nose twitched as he tested the air.

"He half knows we are here, but still has some doubt." Pawonto spoke so low the boy was not sure he heard it or thought it. "Are you ready?"

He turned to his father and smiled excitedly, his black eyes flashing. They stood up into the full view of the buck.

The deer instantly stiffened to full attention. Neither man moved for they wanted the buck to go straight away from them down into the valley and not around the side of the mountain where he could hide in the junipers and be nearly impossible to drive out.

One of the does took a couple of tentative, cautious steps toward them. Both men stood stock still. She stamped her front feet and snorted out a lungful of air, tying to startle the strangers into moving so she could tell if they were enemies or not.

Pawonto raised his arm and waved it over his head. That was too much for the buck and he sprang down the hill. The does and fawns instantly followed.

The boy leaped forward in high spirits, feeling as if he could run forever. He floated along after the herd as they bounded downward through the waist-high brush. They raced south down the west side of the valley between the dry watercourse and the rimrock.

Five miles later the herd crossed the gravel bed of the stream. The buck and one dry doe continued south while the remaining does with their fawns turned east and disappeared into a thick pocket of willow.

Escape from the valley in the south was by a narrow pass, carved by the stream in its intermittent spring flows. The big stag had never been through the winding ravine and he stopped and looked down its length for a long moment. Then he glanced backward and saw the tenacious pursuer closing the distance between them.

Whirling left to the east, he began the long run back up the east side of the valley. He would not be driven from his territory.

The sun crept up its heated arc. Seeking a minute rest, the deer darted down into a bushy draw. After two rocks thrown by the boy crashed down near him, the buck bounded out without the doe and fled up the valley.

The boy's body was slippery with sweat and the salty brine

dripped from the soaked headband and stung his eyes. His legs, which two hours before had felt as if they could run all day, were tightening up on him. Then his second-wind surge of strength eased his breathing and his feet grew light again.

He quickened his pace and gained upon and crowded the deer. His fear increasing, the stag deserted the flat and began to climb toward a break in the rimrock to try to find escape on the tableland above.

"Slow down. Slow down. You are driving him out of the valley," said Pawonto softly to his son from his observation station high on a point of the mountain.

Recognizing what the deer planned, the boy pulled back. The deer, seeing this, stopped fighting the scree of the steep slope and plunged back into the valley. And there, half hidden in the dry grass, the boy found the pile of black round pellets and damp spot where the deer had relieved himself. Remembering what his father had said, that when the deer empties himself the chase is more than half over, the boy measured his remaining strength and was nearly certain he could outlast the deer.

Deer and boy, breathing through dry, open mouths, raced over the rocks, through the brown grass and the stiff, stabbing brush. The deer more and more doubled back and switched direction at sharp angles. Often the boy was trailing the scant sign on the dry ground. No longer did he try to rush the deer, but tried only to hang on, finish the chase, and wear his quarry out.

The deer looked backward again and his pursuer, more stubborn than the wolf, still clung to his trail. He straightened his course and headed directly for the thick junipers high on the side of the mountain. In that shadowy thicket the buck thought he could elude the human.

Pawonto, from his vantage point, saw and understood the

strategy of the buck. *Now! Now! You have him! Catch him on the uphill climb! Run him into the ground!*

As if hearing the silent encouragement, the boy increased his pace, his lungs straining and jaded legs driving. Pawonto sprang up and hurried to intercept the boy and deer and see the kill. The race was nearly over.

Noiselessly Pawonto trotted along beneath the juniper trees. In the bottom of a ravine angling across the lower slope of the mountain, he found the big stag at bay, his sharp, bone-white antlers lowered threateningly at the boy. Though his sides heaved with exhaustion, the stag's alert eyes followed every movement of his enemy, waiting for that one opportunity when he could lunge forward and impale his small adversary on the spearlike tines.

The rock was heavy, but the boy held it above his head and cautiously circled the buck. Carefully watching the wicked antlers, he gradually worked in closer. Suddenly he lunged in, stopped four feet short of the waiting and braced points and crashed the rock down, snapping off the three point side of the antlers at the base. He grabbed up another rock and struck again, driving the buck to the ground.

Instantly the boy hurled himself upon the deer's head, pinning it to the ground with his full weight. The buck struggled to rise, but its neck could not lift the boy. Holding a death grip with one hand, the young hunter jerked his knife out and stabbed again and again into the thick hair on the throat. The sharp point found the hot, pumping carotid artery, and the blood spurted out, sprinkling the juniper needles with bright red drops.

Pawonto slipped away a few yards and returned, stepping noisily on the dead twigs; he would never tell his son he had been close at hand to help, had he been needed.

"You have done well, my son. I am proud of you. Rest now

while I get your mother and the horse, and we will skin this
great buck."

Pawonto returned shortly and the family, laughing in high
spirits, dressed the deer. The mother and father told the boy
what an excellent runner he was and how wisely he had run
the chase.

"I will tan this big skin and make you a warrior's jacket,"
promised his mother.

French, his four men, and the captive girl rode down over
the rim of the rocky canyon at the lower end of Mormon Valley and hurried north along the dry stream bed. They had
been riding hard since daybreak; by nightfall they planned to
be at the last relay of horses and then on the fresh mounts to
make a fast ride on into the badlands camp.

The riders traversed the valley without stopping and entered the junipers. Shorty led, holding a course a little high
on the side of the mountain so as to shorten the distance, for
the girl sagged in the saddle and needed the long, hard travel
to come to an end. Trotting their horses silently on the carpet
of needles beneath the trees, they crossed a small rise and
turned along the lip of a ravine.

Pawonto heard the muffled thump of the horses' hooves
approaching along the rim above. "Quiet! Listen!" he hissed,
pointing in the direction of the sound.

The woman stopped rolling the deerskin and looked upward toward the top of the ravine. Silently the boy stood up
from where he had been resting on the ground.

Pawonto heard the clank of an iron horseshoe on a rock
and knew that unless his people had stolen a white man's
horse, the approaching riders were his enemies. He was afraid,
for he knew the bottom of the ravine was the worst possible
place for his family to be caught.

The riders, white men in big hats, broke free of the screening junipers and looked down from the top of the bank on to the Indians. They jerked their horses to a halt.

Pawonto swept his arm past his son and stabbed a finger at the horse. "Take the horse and ride. Hurry! Ride!" he ordered.

The boy hesitated. After all he was a warrior now, and warriors did not run.

"Go! Go!" Pawonto's urgent cry left no room for argument or hesitation.

The lithe young Indian sprang toward the horse, bounded up on a knee-high rock, and launched himself onto the pack bags still strapped to the horse's back. He rammed his heels into the animal's flanks and slapped the long neck sharply with his hand. The horse leaped away.

Pawonto snatched up his bow and arrows, grabbed the woman by the hand, and broke into a run down the arroyo bottom.

"Kill them! They've seen us!" yelled French. "You," he pointed toward Storms, "shoot the boy. The rest of you help me get those two."

Storms jerked his rifle free and jumped to the ground. The boy, bent far over the horse's neck and digging his heels into the horse's flank, drew rapidly away. Each lunge of the horse brought him closer to safety. He heard no shots or sounds of pursuit. At the break in the arroyo wall he whirled his horse to the right, up the steep trail. The gunman sighted along the rifle barrel. The front sight searched for and found the rider, and then both sight and boy settled into alignment in the V-notch of the rear sight and Storms squeezed the trigger.

The horse reared up as if pulled from behind by an invisible lasso, fell backward onto the young rider, crushing the ribs of his chest and the life from him in one long, piercing wail. Both continued to roll and tumble until they struck the arroyo bottom.

Pawonto darted in under a large juniper and hesitated a second to reconnoiter. The crash of the rifle and the death cry of his son, funneled to him by the vertical walls of the ravine, pierced his soul. A great sob convulsed his powerful chest. With a savage grip on his woman's hand, he sprang from the hiding limbs of the tree and raced away between the banks.

Three members of the gang, followed some distance behind by Shorty and Beth, spurred along the ravine top trying to keep the running Indians in view in the rock and trees of the bottom.

"Shoot them! Shoot!" yelled French above the rattle and thump of the horses' hooves. He fired his six-gun rapidly at the flash of a human below.

Perrine and Acosta joined in, shooting quickly one shot after another. The bullets tore downward, smashed into the rocks, and ricocheted away, howling their deadly song through the brush.

The woman fell and her hand tore loose from Pawonto's grasp. He slid to a stop and sprang back to kneel beside her. The smooth brownness of her throat was ripped open; a ricocheting bullet, a tumbling, misshapen chunk of lead had struck her in the side of the neck and sawed a great, gaping wound. Her stricken eyes searched his face. The soft lips moved, trying to speak, but the mutilated throat could utter no sound. Then the loving brown eyes went blank in death.

His son and woman were dead. Pawonto screamed his terrible anguish. His scream turned to hate and then to a savage challenge. He jumped erect, fitted an arrow to the powerful bow, and pulled it to full draw. His mighty muscles hardened and he held the draw.

Perrine sped up to the edge of the ravine. The Indian man stood there in the open, erect and looking at him. For a split second, Perrine did not see the bow, and then it quivered as the mighty tension on the draw string was released. He tried to duck out of the way, but the arrow already rushed toward him. The hard flint point slipped in between his ribs, tore through his lungs and shattered against the heavy bones of his spine.

French, trailed closely by Acosta, was practically on top of Perrine when he stopped at the ravine. As Perrine fell from his horse, French fired quickly down on the Indian, knocking him to his knees. Pawonto struggled to rise and French shot him twice more, driving him flat into a brown, lifeless mound beside the woman.

Storms hurried up, followed by Shorty and Beth.

"You beast! That was not necessary. What harm could they do to you?" Beth cried to French, looking down at the two lifeless forms.

"They saw us and could tell the posse," answered French.

"That's not true! They would have hidden from the posse same as they tried to do from us," rejoined Beth, tears in her eyes. "You killed them just for the fun of it."

French shrugged his shoulders and looked away.

"That buck sure put that arrow clean through Perrine," said Storms. "Bet he never knew what hit him." Then in a barbed voice he asked French, "Want to give him the same kind of burial we gave Otley?"

French ignored the taunt. He retrieved Perrine's handgun and holster and his rifle and put them on the packhorse.

"Let's ride," said French and kicked his horse away from the lip of the ravine. He motioned with his head for Shorty to take the lead. "How long before we get to Gillespie and McClung and the next relay of horses?"

"Less than an hour," replied Shorty.

"Then let's get there."

CHAPTER 13

Mormon Valley baked in the hot noonday sun. It was an ancient basin, some eight miles wide and two to three hundred feet deep. Located on the most extreme northern edge of the large lava field, it had been threatened by invading tongues of molten rock. But the lava, far extended from the volcanic fissure that birthed it, halted at the very edge of the basin. Those hardened lava tongues, now broken and eroded, rimmed the valley on three sides. A quartz-rich granite mountain made the remaining side.

The valley had not escaped unwounded. A lava dike, a great igneous sheet of liquid rock, had been thrust vertically upward through the earth's crust, cutting completely across the belly of the basin from side to side. That savage wound was now marked by a massive black scar of solidified basalt.

A stream, the same age as the valley, once flowed down from the high slopes of the mountain. It had beat at the dike and after several years broke through it and continued to scour the valley. But the stream was dead now, temporarily, lying dry and dusty in the drought.

Peter and Skinner and their four horses halted at the rim of the basin.

The younger man led, following the trail of the five outlaws and their captive. He glanced back at Skinner riding slumped

in the saddle, head down, and eyes closed. The last eighteen
hours had taken a heavy toll from him. In the one-hundred-
degree temperature, Peter sweated slightly, but Skinner's face
was dry and pale.

Peter looked down into the basin, examining it intently,
searching desperately for a sign that might indicate water.
But the brown saucerlike depression held no green vegetation
except for a few willows adjacent to the stream course. The
scattered junipers looked brown and lifeless in the burning
sunlight.

The sooty ribbon of the durable basalt dike was draped
across the land and stood above the soft older rock by three to
four feet. From the top of the basin rim, it seemed to Peter to
be a giant black snake creeping through the yellow bunch
grass.

Peter checked the map again, then guided the way into the
basin. The heat increased as they dropped down into the bottom and the slight breeze that had been blowing on top died
away completely. He stopped on the bank of the stream
channel.

"We should be close to where the map shows the water to
be. You rest here in the shade of the willows while I try to
find it," said Peter, as he helped Skinner down.

The badly dehydrated man staggered into the sparse
shadow of the spindly brush with its dwarfed leaves and sat
down. He looked at the dry stream. "Better make it fast." His
voice was a hoarse rasp through lips swollen and cracked.

An hour later Peter returned. "Nothing, absolutely nothing. There isn't a damp spot or a speck of green grass anywhere around."

Skinner raised up from where he had been lying. "What
kind of a symbol did your dad use on the map—a spring, a
creek, or just what?"

"He used the sign for a running stream with a mark through it."

"What does that mean?"

"I don't know. I thought he told me all the marks."

"Maybe he meant there was only water at certain times of the year. And this year has been a hell of a drought."

Peter squatted down beside Skinner to rest. He felt a little light-headed himself in the terrible heat.

"It'd be a hell of a story to tell if Skinner was to die of thirst in a country he was raised up in, even if it was a part he had never been in," whispered Skinner. His attempt at a chuckle was a painful series of dry convulsions of his throat.

Peter looked at Skinner, but did not see any humor in dying for lack of water. He wondered if the thirsty man was becoming delirious.

They lay in the scanty shade and panted like dogs. A small gray lizard with a purple ring around its neck scampered from one shady spot to another larger one under the edge of a rock. In the perfectly dead, still air, the willows stood riven in place, their small elongated leaves curled halfway closed to lessen the loss of precious moisture.

Skinner staggered to his feet and stood swaying. Peter stood up quickly and moved close to him in case he needed help.

"Peter, I'm a little dizzy and can't see too well. Is there a high place near here we can climb up on?"

"How high?"

"Oh, anything, just a few feet tall so we can see the bottom of the valley and the rims."

"Yes, over there a couple of hundred yards is a higher place, maybe a twenty- or thirty-foot mound."

"Does it have a good view?"

"Yeh, I think it would have."

"Then get my glass out of the pack and let's get on top of the high ground."

Skinner made it on the level by himself, but Peter had to help him up the side of the low ridge of dirt and rock paralleling the course of the stream.

The big man turned to the south and spread his legs. "Let's both check every possible place where water could exist. We must find a fresh green spot. Now what do you see?"

Peter rotated slowly as he methodically worked the view of the telescope around the valley.

"It's hard to see with all the heat waves making everything move," he commented. "But I don't see any green, just the brown bunch grass and the gray sagebrush. Maybe you could call those junipers green, but they don't mean any water is there."

"No, they don't. Look carefully now, at the walls of the valley where there is higher country above it. Look right into any cracks or gullies in those lava rims and specially in underneath them."

Peter did as directed. "There is nothing—nothing close enough I can see even with the telescope," he reported, lowering the glass from his eye.

"You saw absolutely nothing green?"

"Only the willows down near where the dry stream bed cuts through the black strip of rock where we were laying."

Skinner cackled in half-delirious laughter and his big hand swung swiftly around and grabbed Peter's shoulder in a vise-like grip.

"That's it! The willows! The stream bed and the willows. Let's get down there."

"But it's dry—just dust and rock. My dad told me willow roots can go down fifty feet after water."

Skinner was already stumbling down the slope toward the

channel and did not answer. At the intersection of the dike and the lowest point in the center of the stream channel, he sat down.

Peter hurried up to him. "Skinner, we can't dig fifty feet even if we had shovels, which we don't."

"Don't have to. Look, see how the course of the stream bends back and forth, kind of meanders above this rock, cutting across it; and how over there below, it runs straight?"

As Peter nodded, he continued, "That means that somewhere buried down there, this rock is like a damn and all the underground water must pile up against it and then flow over the top. The problem is we can't tell how deep it is. You can see the sand and rock are laid down in a gap which goes right through the lava. But there must be water below where we are sitting. Start digging."

Peter hurried to the packs and fished out their tin drinking cups. He returned and gave one to Skinner. They both began to dig.

"How deep would you guess it is down to the water?" Peter asked.

Skinner did not answer. His strokes with the cup were ineffectual and he seemed to have lapsed into a half coma after the spurt of energy at the possible discovery of water.

"You all right?" asked Peter, concerned at the man's lack of response.

"Barely," muttered Skinner in his dry, raspy voice. "Don't take too long." He toppled forward onto his face.

Peter turned his friend's face out of the sand and then again dug as fast as he could. But he only found the dry, crumbly sand and an occasional round rock. He was down three feet when the bank gave way, and with a puff of dust, a bushel of sand slid into the hole, filling it a third full again.

"It's starting to slough in. I'm going to have to make the

top of the hole bigger and start again," he commented to the motionless bulk of his friend.

The slumped figure stirred slightly, but there was no answer.

"Better let me help you into what shade there is," suggested Peter.

"Dig, just dig. I think I can crawl up the bank by myself and find the shade." Slowly and laboriously, Skinner inched himself into the shadows cast by the willows.

Hands raw, Peter grubbed out a pit just upstream of the dike. At four feet he found the damp sand. He tried to yell in joy, but could not get the sound from his dry throat. For the first time he realized that not only Skinner was dying from thirst.

He tried again. "Skinner, it's getting damp! It's wet!"

Feverishly he tossed the cups of sand from the pit. Then he hit cracked and eroded bedrock. There were more rocks than sand now and the cracks in the bedrock were wedged full and tight with pebbles. He pried them loose and the crevices filled slowly with water.

Finally, with a half cup of water, he climbed from the hole and stumbled to the side of Skinner. Lifting the white face, he shoved the cup against the cracked lips.

"Drink! It's water. Drink, man, wake up and drink!" He tried to pour the water into the mouth, but it ran from the loose lips into the dirt. Peter slapped him smartly on the side of the face. "Damn you, don't waste it."

Skinner's eyes flickered. "That you, Peter?"

"Yes, and this is water, wet and cool. Drink."

The swollen lips gaped open and the cool water washed into the parched throat.

"That's good," said Peter. "Just rest and I'll be back with more in a minute."

The sun worked its way across the blue sky while Peter

labored at collecting the water. Periodically, he gave Skinner another cupful and drank several himself. While he waited for more water to seep into the hole, he enlarged the drainage area and rounded the bottom so all the water settled in one place. Soon he was getting a cupful every two minutes or so.

Skinner's body moisture was restored and he slept under the willows. Peter's needs were tended to and he began to accumulate water for the horses.

They could not be allowed into the pit for they would tear down the banks and choke off the water, already coming in too slowly. But by cupping the water into the canteens and then into his hat and holding it for the horses, he had provided them with nearly two gallons each by nightfall.

He continued to work late into the night accumulating the precious liquid for the horses. About midnight he fell into an exhausted sleep on the sand of the creek bottom.

He had not killed the mountain lion after all. It had his arm in its mouth and was biting him. Peter tried to pull away and could not. He came awake with a start, with Skinner kneeling beside him vigorously shaking his arm.

"You okay?" Skinner asked, his haggard face and bloodshot eyes concerned.

"Yeah," Peter answered and sat stiffly up. "I'm sore all over."

"So am I. Every muscle I've got aches. How much water is the hole making?"

"Last night before I went to sleep it was making a cupful every couple of minutes. The flow seemed to increase after it got dark."

"I've noticed springs make more water at night. I think the willows and other water-loving trees that have their roots down in it don't pull the water up to the leaves and waste it when it is cooler. Let's take a look to see how much water is in your well."

Peter grabbed up the canteens and tin cup and followed Skinner. Careful not to loosen the precariously balanced sand walls, he stepped down into his shallow well and balanced himself on a flat rock he had placed there to keep his feet out of the water.

During the night while he slept, the underground stream had fed the well, and three or four inches of clear water covered the bottom.

He dipped a fresh cup and handed it to Skinner who greedily drank it. "Another," he requested and drank that one and a third. "That's enough for awhile," he said. "I'll check the horses."

Peter drank a full cup and began to ladle the liquid into the inch-size necks of the canteens. As he tried to scoop up the last of the water, two pebbles, the size of small marbles and wedged in the cracks of the bedrock, got in the way. They were dull, brass-yellow and did not grate on the metal cup the way quartz did. He pried them loose with his fingers and, doubting his sudden imaginings as to what they might be, dropped them into his pocket.

"All the canteens are full," Peter called. "We're ready to give the horses more water." Heavily laden, with the canteens hanging on their long straps thumping and bumping, he climbed out of the hole.

Skinner came to meet him and helped carry the water to the horses. Jerking off their hats, they poured them full of water and held them for the horses.

"They still look gaunt. How much did you give them last night?"

"About a third enough."

"Then let's fill them up and ride easy for awhile."

"It will take some time. The water is coming in better than yesterday, but still slow."

"That's okay, I don't want to cut it as close as we did this last time. One more day without water and I might have begun to feel it," he grinned at Peter through sore lips.

"I had a thirsty spell or two myself," agreed Peter. He dug into his pocket and pulled out the pebbles. "Do you know anything about rocks? Any chance these are gold?" He held them out to Skinner.

He took them, rolled them around in the palm of his hand, and then bit down gently on one. "It's a gold nugget all right! Where did you find it?" Skinner's voice rose a notch with excitement.

"The bottom of my well has several of them," answered Peter quickly, shoving his thumb in the direction of the creek and his eyes firing up. "They are lying on the bottom and some are stuck in the cracks of the rock."

"Son-of-a-gun, you may have found a gold glory hole," chuckled Skinner.

Peter, laughing with him, rushed to the pit dug so laboriously and jumped down inside. "Here's a nugget, and another, and another!" Then he was very quiet as he scrounged in the bottom and filled the tin cup with the precious yellow metal.

His head popped above the rim of the sump. "Look at this heaping cup of gold! And is it ever heavy!" he exclaimed excitedly.

Skinner reached down and Peter dumped the tin full of nuggets into his cupped hands. Skinner sat on his haunches, looking at the nuggets. They ranged in size from that of a pea to that of a cherry. Some were nearly round and others flattened and misshapen; all showed the beating they had taken in their tumbling trip down from the quartz mountain lying to the north.

"Peter, earlier on this hunt you asked how you could square yourself with the law about robbing the bank. Well, money has marvelous ways to help a man get what he wants. With enough of this yellow stuff and the help of John Manderfield, you just might make it."

Peter looked up at the big red-headed man and smiled happily, "God! I hope so."

While they waited for more water to seep in, they uncovered fresh bedrock and the treasure lying immediately on top of it and loaded the cup nearly full again. Peter opened his knife and dug out the nuggets jammed into the cracks of the bedrock and finished filling the cup. From the sand and rocks thrown out during the previous day's digging, they found a few more yellow hunks and added them to the hoard, heaping the top of the cup.

Carefully Peter piled the treasure trove on a flat rock and divided it into two equal mounds of yellow nuggets. "Take your pick. Which pile do you want?"

"You found them and they're yours," answered Skinner, shaking his head in the negative.

Peter looked him in the eye for a long moment and said matter-of-factly, "Do you remember when you said you and me together would kill all the gang that stole Beth? Well, that made us full partners. You take half or I'll throw them out there in the brush and lose them."

Skinner returned Peter's stare, and then a pleased grin spread across his face. "I'll take it because I also feel we're full partners and I would've given you half had I been the one who found it." He reached out and scooped the nearest pile into his hat, realizing as he did so that he felt Peter was more like a younger brother than a partner.

"Good," said Peter, grinning back. "Now what do we do with the rest that's not dug yet? The bottom of that creek must be covered with a thousand times this much gold."

"Let's cover it, and after we get our job done and get Beth back, we'll come here again with tools and dig every nugget."

"We'll be rich as old King Midas," laughed Peter.

They finished watering the horses and filled the canteens. Scraping and kicking, they filled the hole with sand and rock. Skinner led his horses down onto the creek bottom and walked them over the fresh digging a few times.

"That's good enough. No one is going to find it way out here," said Skinner.

CHAPTER 14

Peter and Skinner rode up out of Mormon Valley and entered the junipers strewn on the flank of the quartz mountain. The horses walked slowly, their stomachs so ballooned with water that they looked like pregnant mares. In the late afternoon sun, horses and riders threw long dark shadows ahead of them.

Skinner, leading, pulled up quickly. "Look down there," he said in a low voice, pointing to the dead horse half lying on the Indian boy.

"Somebody shot the horse. I can see the bullet hole," whispered Peter. "Now why would they do that?"

Skinner shook his head and reined away. "Some people got to kill. From the looks of the boy, he has been dead a couple of days. Let's move on, because we got to hurry. We're far behind."

A moment later the stallion snorted and tossed his head at something lying in the brush. Skinner pulled him up and looked down on Perrine, the shaft of the arrow protruding from the bloated body. He looked away, his glance falling over the rim of the canyon where he saw the bodies of the two Indians in the arroyo bottom.

"It looks like the gang killed the whole family. But the buck got one of them first."

"Damn poor trade, if you ask me," said Peter.

"It helps us. That's one less gun against us."

Skinner hurried them away from the mountain and the
dead. The shade of the junipers was left far behind, and they
entered a large expanse of small, round hills. Nearly all the
larger ones were capped with black lava bonnets, which in
some instances made up more than half of the hill's bulk. In
the washes between the hills, sagebrush grew in narrow
fingers.

Peter thought of the bag of gold he had stashed in the saddlebags along with the money from the bank. The bank loot
must be returned, but first the gold of Mormon Valley had to
be dug, or at least enough for him to do as Skinner said—try
to buy himself out of the deep trouble he was in. But even before that, Beth had to be freed and returned home to her
grandfather.

On the shady side of nearly every hill, in the jumble of rock
that had tumbled down from the lava cap rocks, alert rock
chucks lay and inspected the intruders as they passed. Skinner
saw the brown-furred animals, their long, low-slung bodies
flattened against the dirt of their dens. With keen eyes watching every movement, the large rodents gradually backed into
the safety of their nests as the riders drew abreast, then returned to the surface once they were gone.

Skinner halted, removed his hat, and began to wipe the
sweat from his forehead with his shirt sleeve. Without turning, he spoke to Peter in a low voice, "Can you hear me?"

"Yes," answered Peter, looking quizzically at Skinner's
back.

"Very slowly look at that small hill ahead on the right.
There has been rock chucks in the mouth of every den for
several miles, but not in the dens on that hill. Somebody is up
on top."

"I don't see them."

"They're up there. We are already in rifle range so we can't turn back or they'll start shooting."

"How many do you think there are?"

"One or two," answered Skinner. "We can't let them escape to warn the others for they might hurt Beth."

"I'm game for anything. What's your plan?" asked Peter, untying the lead rope of the gray from the pommel in preparation to ride or shoot or both.

"When I give the word, ride like hell to the back side of the hill. Try to keep whoever it is from getting away. Kill them if you have to, but it would be better if they could talk. There are some questions we need answered."

"Where will you be so I don't shoot you by mistake?"

"Going around the north side to head them off if they go that way."

"I'm ready."

"Go!" yelled Skinner.

Peter dropped the gray's lead rope, swung his horse right, and spurred hard. The crack of a rifle at a distance sounded above the pound of the horse's iron-shod hooves. He did not hear the bullet.

The roan charged in a dead flat run. Bent low over the horse's neck, Peter darted through the sagebrush and across the grassy spaces in between.

A bullet whizzed past the tip of his nose. Then he was in the shadow of the cap rock, protected from shots from above. That lasted but a few seconds and he burst into the open again.

Directly ahead of Peter, a man on foot, jinking like a frightened jack rabbit, raced through the waist-high brush. Peter saw the figure for a fleeting glance, then dropping down in a swale, lost sight of him. He stood up in the stirrups to get the man back in view and urged his horse up toward the peak of the ridge.

Swiftly Peter crested the top of the hill. The man stood ready, his rifle instantly centering on him. Peter's heart shrank in realization that at this short range the man could not miss. He was as good as dead. As the thought flashed through Peter's mind, the man winced and crumpled into the brush.

Throwing a hurried look, Peter saw Skinner sitting the stallion, the smoking rifle still at his shoulder. He let a deep sigh of relief escape him as he marveled at Skinner's skill to place the bullet as he had done, for it was an extremely long shot and from horseback. He rode on across the hill to where the man had fallen into the brush and dismounted.

Peter searched the man, stood up and called to Skinner, "He's dead and won't be answering any questions. Had some papers on him. Seems his name is McClung, Frank McClung."

Skinner nodded his understanding, swiveling his eyes watchfully over the sagebrush and lava-rock terrain surrounding them.

Peter mounted his horse and spoke to Skinner. "Let's ride up to the point of the hill where this fellow was laying in ambush for us and see if there's anyone else."

"Might be wiser and safer to ride the other way, out in the direction that fellow was running, and see how many horses we can find. If there's more than one, we'll come back and get whoever else is up there."

Peter nodded at the good sense in Skinner's suggestion. They closed the distance between them as they angled in on the direction the man had been heading.

"That's one I owe you," said Peter as they came close. "Thanks for blasting him. He had me dead to rights and would have gotten me for sure."

"Just paying you back for that drink of water yesterday," laughed Skinner.

At the base of the hill they found one horse and turned it loose.

Skinner measured the height of the sun, its red sphere already touching the horizon. "Tomorrow morning we will find their camp."

"How do you know?"

"That would-be bushwhacker didn't have a bedroll, so he planned to return to his camp tonight. Let's find a place to camp ourselves. We don't want to blunder into the gang in the dark."

The lookout for the day, Gillespie, rode into camp an hour after dark. He unsaddled his horse, removed the bridle, and slapped the animal away to graze in the meadow surrounding the spring. Without saying a word, he joined the other outlaws lounging around the fire in the middle of the grove of cottonwoods. He poured himself a cup of coffee from the pot sitting in the edge of the hot embers and squatted down and began to sip at the steaming liquid.

French felt moderately safe. It was the end of the first full day in the badlands hideout. The gang had traveled swiftly, and there had been no sign of pursuit. After night had fallen, he had allowed a small cooking fire to be built deep in the patch of trees so the flames could not be seen from any distance.

He watched Gillespie noisily suck at the hot coffee. "Did you see anything?" he asked.

"Two lizards, a rattlesnake, and a stinkbug," answered Gillespie, without seeming to care who had asked the question.

"How about McClung—see anything of him?" asked French.

Gillespie shook his head. "I looked long and hard just before dark and didn't see any sign of him."

"I told you to wait on him and both of you come into camp together. Did you hear any shooting?"

"Nope, I heard nothing. But McClung might have gone far enough along our back trail that I couldn't have heard a shot even if there had been one. I waited nearly an hour after dark before I started back. And anyway, McClung acts half-Indian and doesn't care to sleep out without his bedroll. I like my blankets."

French stood up and called out loud enough for all to hear, "Doesn't look like McClung is coming in tonight, but let's talk anyway. We've had a full day to rest. Old Manderfield should be back from Denver with the money, so it's time to go after it."

All four of the men and Beth, who sat in the edge of the shadows, looked at the Canadian.

"Suppose something has happened to McClung?" asked Storms.

"Nothing we can do to search for him on a night this dark," said French. "We'll post a guard all night just in case someone got past him."

"What's the plan?" asked Storms.

"Gather 'round and let me draw a map so we'll all know what we're talking about," said French. He smoothed out a spot on the dry dirt with his hand and picked up a short piece of stick.

"Now here is the alkali." On the ground he drew a large oval, slightly longer in its north to south direction. "And here are the badlands, and we're about here." He continued to scratch the ground. "Along here on the east side of the desert is lava rimrock and about here is a finger of it extending out a quarter mile or so into the alkali.

"This finger is eight or ten miles north of Westfall and you all can find it easy. Tomorrow morning just at first light, Shorty, the girl and me will head south along the eastern edge of the alkali. About here, Shorty will split off and take the girl up to the top of the lava and wait. I'll go on to the Manderfield ranch and leave directions for the old man as to where and when to bring the money."

French ceased talking and swung a penetrating look from one gang member to another to see how they were taking the plan.

"That's all fairly much as we talked about it a few days back, except for you and Shorty going off by yourselves with the girl," said Storms. "What about the rest of us?"

"We still don't know but what there ain't someone right behind us hot on our trail," said French. "To be sure we got time to get the money, you, McClung when he gets here, Acosta, and Gillespie stay here most of tomorrow. Put out a lookout, same as today. Then late in the day, ride south and meet us where Shorty will have the girl. I'll get the money in the evening and we'll all meet and split the money about dark."

"How are you going to get the money without someone following you when you pick it up?" asked the cautious Shorty.

"I'm going to make Manderfield bring it to me way out on the flat alkali where I can see a rider for miles. I'll put up a tall stake with a flag on it so he can find it and he will leave the money there just before dark. After he leaves, I'll pick up the loot and come to where you all are." French hoped the wary Shorty would not figure out his true plan to have the old man deliver the money in the afternoon instead of at dark. With that earlier timing and hard riding, he could find Shorty and the girl, kill the tricky little bastard, take his fresh horse, and be long gone with the girl before Storms and the rest of the gang showed up.

French continued, "We'll put the girl on a horse and let her find her own way home. After that we'll have all night to go our own ways and be miles away by daylight."

Beth jumped up, stepped into the light of the fire, and faced French. "You liar. You would never divide the money with the others even if you got it. And I don't think you will let me go, either."

French stood up, his face flushing and black eyes savage. "Damn you, woman, you don't know what you are talking about," he rasped. Suddenly he moved forward and slapped her harshly on the side of the face. His hard, calloused hand crushed the small blood vessels beneath the soft skin, and the spot turned rapidly red.

She staggered, but caught her balance and remained standing, tears of rage and pain filling her eyes.

Storms climbed to his feet, tense and poised, with his hand touching the butt of his six-gun. In the shadow cast by the flickering flame of the fire, his eyes were buried in black pits beneath the ridges of his eyebrows like the vacant sockets of a skull.

"Don't hit her again," he warned. "Women are for lovin' and not for beatin'."

On the opposite side of the fire, Shorty's hand slipped into the darkness of his right side. The alert French saw the small man's move.

"Storms, you have a name as a gunfighter, but I believe I can outdraw you," said French. He searched for the man's eyes in the dark holes of his face, wanting to read them.

"It don't make a damn what you believe. So I'm telling you if you hit her again, you'll have to prove you're faster than me. I haven't liked the stealing of a woman from the start, and I've had some of the same thoughts as the girl."

French's hand twitched with eagerness to start the gun play. With Storms dead, that would make one less gun after him when he vamoosed with the ransom money. But then, even if he did gun Storms, he was sure Shorty would kill him before he could turn and nail him.

"Oh, hell! In two days we'll be dividing seventy-five thousand dollars, so why fight," said French, relaxing his stance and giving a weak chuckle.

Beth looked at Shorty, but he refused to meet her eyes. He knew she was questioning why he had not come to her aid and he wasn't about to try to explain there was absolutely nothing to be gained by challenging French after he had already hit her. Except it just might get him killed. And anyway, she shouldn't have called French a liar.

But Shorty also believed French would not divide the money, and he began to lay his own plans to get his share.

CHAPTER 15

With the wide brims of their hats shading their eyes from the early morning sun, Peter and Skinner looked down from the last easternmost extremity of the lava cap rock of the high plateau and inspected the Honeycombs Badlands lying a thousand feet below. The inhospitable and nearly impassable sweep of rock hills and sharp rock pinnacles forming the cells of the imaginary honeycombs stretched before them, curving slowly to the south in a giant arc twenty miles wide and thirty miles long. Pressing tightly against it on the south lay the gray-white Alvord Desert.

The badlands had been formed by the erosion of a great blanket of volcanic debris that a hundred thousand years before had been exploded with great violence upon the land. Wind and water carved and sculptured the ash and rock and stained the mass with splotches of deep reds and browns. Like a giant scab of crusted blood on pale flesh, the somber crescent of the badlands capped the north end of the flour-white desert.

Trotting their horses where they could, the two men hurried down the game trail that zigzagged back and forth across the steep slope below the rimrock. Reaching the bottom, Skinner took the lead again, following the trail. They penetrated the west end of the badlands, easily unraveling the now-familiar pattern of the outlaw gang's effort to hide their sign. The heat built rapidly in the dusty arroyo bottoms though it was still early morning.

"Going to be a scorcher," said Peter, breaking the silence for the first time since they took to the saddle at daybreak.

Skinner nodded agreement at the obvious as he pulled his mount to a stop. "What does your map show for water out that way?" he asked, pointing to the center of the rocky spires of the badlands.

Peter pulled the dusty, sweat-stained map from the saddle-bag and unfolded it over the saddle in front of him. Skinner guided his horse back beside him.

"There's two springs," said Peter, stabbing his finger at a pair of symbols on the deerskin map.

"About one hour's ride," estimated Skinner, having grown used to the scale of the map. "Keep your eyes peeled, because they'll surely have a lookout posted." He led off.

Four miles later Skinner found the boot prints in the dust and jerked to a stop. "Must be right on top of the camp," he whispered. "I don't understand why there's no guard out. Let's go from here on foot."

They quickly tied the horses to a stunted juniper and slid their rifles from the scabbards. Skinner looked at Peter and nodded.

"You take the right and I'll take this side. Look it over and meet back here in ten minutes or so and we'll make a plan. Now keep your head down, and no shooting unless absolutely necessary." They separated and moved off silently.

The valley was a couple hundred yards wide and stretched off upstream and downstream farther than Peter could see. A clump of large cottonwood trees marked the site of one of the springs, and a string of much smaller cottonwoods and some willows fingered down the stream channel. Once, by chance,

Peter spotted Skinner stalking the grove of cottonwoods surrounding the spring.

Scattered junipers dotted the space between the cottonwoods and the steep walls of the valley. Silently Peter slipped from one juniper to the next, working slowly downstream toward the second spring.

As he eased along, the channel narrowed for a few hundred feet, then grew more open, and there were a few waist-high boulders lying randomly about. The wind was completely dead. No birds flew about or sat in the trees. The only sound was the grasshoppers, flushed out by Peter's disturbing feet, flapping out of danger with a short, rapid chatter of wings.

"Looking for something?" asked a low voice from Peter's left.

Peter turned slowly, his eyes searching rapidly for the speaker among the junipers and boulders. He found him, standing between two trees calmly watching him, his pistol still in its holster.

The man should not have been there. Up on a lookout, maybe, or at camp, but not here.

"What are you looking for?" asked Storms again, watching the quick flash of surprise sweep over the young man's face. But the surprise disappeared immediately. Storms detected the minute shift of the youth's body in preparation for gun play and for an instant wondered if he had made a mistake in not shooting the stranger on sight.

Storms would have liked to look around the valley for friends of the intruder for he seemed too sure of himself. But his gunman instinct told him not to take his eyes off the fellow or even blink. Then his complete confidence in his skill returned and his pulse quickened in anticipation that the young man might draw against him.

"Wouldn't be looking for a golden-haired girl, would you?" asked Storms.

The man did not answer and Storms's eye recorded another almost invisible preparatory shift of the man's body for action.

Peter examined the unconcerned gunman who stood quietly watching him and realized this man was different and more deadly than all the others he had faced. It showed in his penetrating eyes, his tied-down, well-used gun, and cold, calculating stare.

"Are you going to draw on me?" asked Storms.

Peter started to nod his head, but instead dropped the rifle, stabbed his hand for his six-gun, drew, and fired.

Storms, stunned by the trickery of that false half nod and the speed of the draw, grabbed his own gun with razor-sharp reflex. Something slugged him in the chest and his shot went off mark. As he staggered he made as if to fire again, but before he squeezed off the round, another savage blow to the chest knocked his aim off target. Then the blackness swept across his eyes and he could not see to shoot. The pistol dropped from his lifeless hand.

Peter wiped a thin film of sweat from his forehead with the back of his hand. That had been too close, much too close. He flipped out the cylinder of his six-gun and ejected the two spent shells.

A flicker of movement in the edge of the junipers off to his left caught the corner of Peter's eye. As he whirled to face the new threat, he snapped the cylinder of his gun back into place with only four rounds in it.

Before he could turn completely, a heavy, spinning rifle slug exploded the upper bone of his left arm and plowed into his chest. The chunk of lead slammed him to the ground. He struggled half erect and tried to bring his pistol up. Above his straining labors, he heard someone screaming, "Keep firing! Shoot! Shoot!"

Almost instantly a bullet smashed into Peter's head and another through his heart.

"We got him!" yelled a man jubilantly. "We got the son-of-a-bitch!"

"Ollie, I thought you knew this country, but all you've done is get us lost," said the exasperated sheriff. He rode immediately behind Ollie, the wide brim of his hat pulled low over his eyes to shield them from the bright rays of the sun.

"Nobody knows the badlands well enough but what he gets confused once in awhile," answered Ollie. He realized he had guided the posse into the Honeycombs too far south. For the past four hours they had meandered back and forth, searching for a route north and finding one dead-end arroyo after another. But now he recognized the dry stream bed they had just entered.

"This channel leads right up to the springs, the littler one first. We will be there in less than an hour," said Ollie, relief evident in his voice.

The sheriff only grunted in response. Soon his guess as to where Pipe was headed would be proved right or wrong. If he was correct and they had a little luck, the chase would soon be over; but if wrong, he just might have to return to Westfall and recruit a new posse.

A few minutes later Ollie stopped and pointed to a green patch of cottonwoods about a quarter mile distant, lying in under a tall rock spire that dwarfed them. "There is the smaller spring, where the trees are, and not as far as I thought."

"Which spring is the better camp?" asked the sheriff.

"The upper water. It has more trees and a small meadow. It's just around the bend of the arroyo, not much farther than this one if you cut straight across."

"All right. You fellows find some shade nearby and keep

out of sight. I'll check the upper spring first, and if there is nothing there, I'll swing back past the other one. Won't be gone long." The sheriff dismounted, tied his horse behind one of the small junipers scattered about on the valley bottom, and walked away, hunched down low.

Two of the posse members climbed down and led their horses a few feet away, pressing in close to the junipers to get into their shadow. Buck and Oscar Fettus also dismounted, and Ollie motioned them to come to him. His sharp eyes had seen movement in the edge of the cottonwoods.

"Let's just walk over there to the lower spring and give it a look-see. Save Gumert some time," said Ollie.

Buck looked at Oscar and they edged up closer to their older brother so the other members of the posse could not hear. "Now, Ollie, why would we want to go there without the sheriff?" asked Buck.

A mean grin creased Ollie's jaws. "We just might have some luck and find Pipe there," he said.

"Ollie, let's not do it that way. Let's just wait for the sheriff and play his game," said Buck hopefully.

"No, damn it!" snapped Ollie. "Now tie your horses and stop arguing and take your rifles."

They worked toward the grove of cottonwood trees, slipping from one tree to the next. Ollie had not seen any further movement in the trees after that one brief flutter and began to wonder if he had been mistaken.

Then the voice of a man, speaking quietly and calmly drifted to them. Quickly the three Fettuses dropped to the ground.

"Where's it coming from?" whispered Buck.

Ollie pointed off to the left. "Just over there in the junipers. Let's crawl. Keep your heads down, and don't make one bit of noise."

They snaked silently along a couple dozen yards and peered

around the side of a bushy juniper. Just as Ollie leaned out to get a better view, he saw two men draw on each other. Their shots blended into a crescendo of exploding gunpowder. The muzzle flashes of the six-guns paled the rays of the sun for a split second. The older man staggered and fell, driven to the ground by the younger man's bullets.

Ollie stood up in shocked surprise. Then he motioned his brothers out from behind the tree and whispered in a savage voice, "It's Pipe! Let's get him!" He dropped to his knee so he could do his best shooting.

Skinner lay hidden, watching two men, an Anglo and a Mexican, in the shade of the cottonwood trees pack their bedrolls. Their voices carried plainly to him. There was no sign of Beth or other gang members.

"Do you think French will get the money?" asked Gillespie, the Anglo one of the pair.

The Mexican, Acosta, without looking up from tying the thongs around his blankets, answered, "Will he meet us with the money, is the better question, and will he give the girl back?"

"Yeah, I've been thinking about that, too. The girl called it right, I bet." Gillespie finished packing and lugged the load to his horse. "I hope Storms hurries up and finds his horse. He should've tied him up last night. I want to get to Shorty and the girl before French does."

"I wonder why McClung didn't show up last night?" said Acosta.

"Aw hell, he's always late. He'll catch up," said Gillespie.

Keeping his head down, Skinner was just turning to crawl away when the rattle of three pistol shots, piled one on top of the other, rolled up the arroyo.

"Storms's run into trouble," yelled Gillespie. "Let's get out of here. We're sitting ducks." The two men scrambled for their horses.

Skinner hesitated for a short second, then jumped upright and raised his rifle. With less compunction than he felt shooting wild mustangs, he shot Gillespie as the man swung into the saddle and started to spur down the valley. Acosta, hearing the crack of the rifle, raked his horse the opposite way, up the canyon. He was an easy target and Skinner busted his heart with the first bullet.

Almost immediately the fusillade of rifle shots rang out from down the arroyo. Mingled with it was the half-crazed voice of a man screaming. And not Peter's voice. Skinner turned and ran full speed toward the sound, reloading as he moved.

The crash of shots ended abruptly. In the stillness he heard the voice yell out in glee, "We got him!" At those words, a terrible fear that his new-found friend was dead seared Skinner's mind.

He was close, so he forced himself to slow to a trot. Crouched far over, he came around the curve of the valley to see the Fettus brothers walking slowly up to a man lying on the ground. Ollie kicked the loose-jointed body onto its back.

Skinner saw Peter's ravaged face and screamed. The shrill cry, pained and anguished, smacked against the arroyo walls, ricocheted and echoed through the cottonwoods and junipers.

"You sons-of-bitches! You're going to die! Every one of you! *You're going to die.*" He cinched his torment in and, gripping his rifle, stepped out into the open.

The three Fettuses spun to face him. Skinner threw the rifle up, squeezed the trigger, and shot Ollie through the chest. Oscar stood dumbfounded and did not move. He took a bullet between the eyes. Buck dropped to the ground and sighted along his rifle barrel at Skinner. Like shooting a weasel in the grass, Skinner shot him through the forehead just above the nose.

Skinner ran to Peter and knelt down. Taking the thin face between his hands, he held it and cried, Peter's blood oozing and dripping through his fingers.

CHAPTER 16

Sheriff Gumert, his six-gun drawn, came up cautiously on the area where the last shooting had sounded. He had been greatly disturbed by the sudden flare of gunfire from the two widely separated springs. Before he had reached the upper water, he had seen a man run from it to the second spring and had followed. The third burst of shots, all rifle fire, erupted and ended before he caught up.

The lawman broke free of the junipers blocking his view and found the man he had followed bent over one of several fallen gunmen. Putting his hand over the hammer of his gun to muffle the noise, the lawman cocked his gun. The kneeling figure heard the nearly inaudible click, and with amazing swiftness his hand stabbed out for the rifle lying near his leg in the grass.

"Skinner, what in hell are you doing here?" exclaimed the surprised sheriff, recognizing the ruddy face as the man swung around. The sheriff saw the deep sorrow in Skinner's eyes.

"The Fettuses killed Peter," replied Skinner, standing up.

The sheriff swung a critical eye over the sprawled corpses of the three brothers and the stranger. "And who shot them?" he questioned suspiciously.

Skinner wiped his hands on his pants and Peter's blood

made deep red stains on the dusty Levi's. When he looked up, his eyes were as alert as an eagle's.

"Peter must have finished them off before he died," he suggested.

Jake Jallapi and the remaining members of the posse charged up and reined in. They dismounted hastily and lined up beside the sheriff, facing Skinner.

"Sheriff, that jasper over there is one of the gang that kidnapped Beth Manderfield," said Skinner. "I have been on their trail for four or five days. And now I've got to go after the last of them."

"Just hold it. There are some things here I don't savvy. What's this about the Manderfield girl?"

In brief, terse sentences, Skinner explained the events leading up to his being in the valley. "So you see, I've got to get after them before they harm Beth. And I believe they just might kill her after they get the money."

"I'm not sure the Pipe kid gunned all four of these men. That's a pretty good story to get you away from here before I find out the truth."

Skinner tensed and he measured the three men with hard eyes. All of them had at some time seen the terrible swift violence of which he was capable. None wanted to take him on.

A low moan, barely heard, sounded from the limp form of Ollie. The sheriff looked at Skinner as if telling him to stay put and hurried over to kneel down close to the dying man. Ollie mumbled and the lawman bent his ear close to the pale lips. Ollie mumbled again, then went slack, his head rolling to the side and the dead eyes staring at Skinner.

Sheriff Gumert stood up and looked at Skinner too.

"What did he say?" asked Jake.

Gumert did not answer but continued to eye Skinner, who confronted him with legs slightly spread and hands lightly holding his rifle. The seconds dragged long and heavy.

"I couldn't make out what he was trying to say," said the sheriff at last. "We'll take Skinner's word for what happened."

Skinner did not relax until the lawman holstered his six-gun.

"You'll find two more dead men up at the other spring," said Skinner. "Now, I'm going."

"And those other two are part of the gang that you have been tracking?" asked the sheriff.

"Yep, and there are one or two more of them left. But I can take care of them without any help. You just stay here and bury the dead." He started to walk away, but turned back, removed Peter's gun belt, and picked up the six-gun near his hand. "Sheriff, I'll owe you a favor if you don't bury Peter near those stinking bastards and if you put a rock marker at the head of his grave so I can find it when I come back."

"I'll do that," said Sheriff Gumert.

"There's eight thousand dollars of the bank's money on Peter's packhorse tied at the foot of the hill west of the spring. I'll leave it there for you to pick up," said Skinner.

"No, I'll go with you and get it now," responded the sheriff.

"Do whatever pleases you," said Skinner and walked away toward the place where he and Peter had tied their horses.

The sheriff followed close behind.

Skinner pushed the stallion at a fast clip along the east side of the alkali desert. He had taken all of Peter's gold and the paper money that wasn't the bank's, refusing the sheriff's offer to find Peter's relatives, if any, and send the money to them. Skinner would do that for his friend himself. He subdued his grief, burying it for the moment, and concentrated on the trail and Beth.

The bandits' trail—Skinner made out the tracks of three horses—was easy to follow, for they had made no effort to hide it.

Though it was a day old, he knew it would be short and the outlaws would be at its end. Beth would be there, too. And somehow he had to get her away from them, take her from them without getting her hurt.

Skinner searched out the trail as far ahead as he could on the whitish soil; on the flat, smooth ground, he could often see it for two or three hundred yards.

Miles slipped away behind them, and the stallion's dark coat took on a shiny wet sheen of sweat. The breeze created by the rapid pace fanned Skinner, evaporating part of his perspiration as it formed, cooling him a little.

The trail ahead of Skinner split, two riders going east toward the edge of the desert and the rimrock that lay between it and the mountain. A single rider continued south in the direction of Westfall and the Manderfield ranch. Skinner swung to the east. Beth would be one of the two riders.

His spirits rose. Only one man stood between him and Beth, and only a few miles away at most.

Shorty turned to Beth, who sat on a rock in the shade behind him and motioned her to come to the edge of the rimrock. Seeing the tense look on his face, she hastened up beside him and lay down.

"Who is that?" he asked, pointing down the steep slope leading to the desert. "Don't look like anyone I know."

Beth looked in the direction he indicated. A lone horseman riding a big black was cautiously picking his way up the grade toward them. He disappeared behind a ridge of lava boulders, then reappeared closer. Stopping his horse, the rider shaded his eyes and examined the cap rock where Beth and Shorty lay hidden.

For several minutes he remained motionless except for an occasional slight turn of his head. Then he dropped his arm, wheeled the horse to the right, and vanished behind a pile of rocks that had tumbled down from the rim.

Beth recognized the big body, the familiar drop of the arm and cant of the head. "It's John Skinner!" she cried happily. "I knew he would be the first one to find me!"

"How did he get past all the others?" asked Shorty, disturbed at the nearness of the man and the skill he must have to be that near.

"John probably left them all dead somewhere back there," said Beth, swinging her hand widely, indicating all the hills, valleys, and long distances she had ridden over in the last several days. She was surprised at herself for not feeling any compunction at the very likely death of many members of the outlaw gang.

Shorty watched the rocks behind which the man had ridden. The rider did not reappear, and the minutes passed. Shorty rose to a crouch and backed away from the edge, pulling Beth with him.

She stopped smiling, suddenly realizing the danger John's appearance held for Shorty, and probably for her also, depending on how he reacted to John's presence.

Shorty quickly considered some possible ways to handle the threatening rider. He still held the advantage, for he knew where the man was, or at least where he was a few minutes ago, while his and Beth's location could at the best only be guessed at. But did he still want the money badly enough to try and kill this John Skinner fellow and hold the girl? He looked at Beth, her peeling, sunburned face thin and drawn, and the blue eyes that had never once showed sign of surrender.

"Miss, I'm sorry for all the trouble we have caused you these past days. Your friend is just down there and you are safe. He might not take kindly toward me if he should catch me, so I'm riding out pronto. Try not to feel too badly of me." Shorty released her arm, turned hurriedly and trotted off in his high-heeled boots in the direction of the horses hidden in the rocks.

Beth watched him go and then ran back to the edge of the rim and climbed up on a large rock so she was in full view from below. "John! John Skinner! It's Beth!" she called loudly.

There was no response. "John, it's Beth!" she yelled as strongly as she could, shouting her happiness down across the boulder-strewn slope and out to the edge of the alkali. "Where are you?"

"Right behind you," said a low voice.

Beth whirled, looked at the tall man with the haggard, sad face for an unbelieving second, and then rushed into his arms. He hugged her, pulling her tightly to him, molding the soft woman's body against him.

She tilted her head backward and stretched upward to kiss him on the mouth. His tears wet her lips, and again, for the first time in all those years, she tasted the pleasant, salty flavor of his sadness.

Rocks rattled on the slope a few hundred feet above them. He shoved her roughly away. Shorty, astride his horse and clearly visible, spurred up the incline through the boulder patch stretching around the side of the mountain. Skinner threw his rifle to his shoulder.

Beth grabbed his arm. "Don't shoot him! He helped me. He kept the others from hurting me."

But Skinner shook her off. He fired three rapid shots, so close together they blended into one rippling roar of exploding gunpowder.

Shorty jerked his horse to a dead stop as broken rock and fragments of lead buzzed off the big boulder immediately on his right. The three splashes of gray lead on the rock could all be covered by his hand. He spun his horse around to face down the slope. Jerking off his hat, he whirled it above his head in salute to the expert marksmanship of the man standing near the girl; telling him he understood that those three bullets could have been through his heart. And would be if they ever met again. He wheeled the horse back to the slope and spurred away in a clatter of rock.

"You missed!" exclaimed Beth in surprise.

"Yes, I missed," said Skinner laughing, mocking her with gentle, happy eyes.

He reloaded his rifle and leaned it against a rock. Beth stepped forward and was again engulfed in his arms. They stood, relishing the touch of their bodies and the removal of all barriers between them.

"John, let's go away from here before the leader of the gang comes," said Beth, pulling back to the limit of Skinner's embrace and looking up into his face.

Silently he touched the bruises on her face and the muscles ridged in his jaws. "We will wait for him," he said.

"But he is terrible and I never want to see him again."

"That is exactly what I intend—for you never to be bothered by him again. To be sure of that I will meet him and we will have an understanding. And I must get your grandfather's money back."

Beth knew what he intended to do. "If something happened to you, I couldn't stand it."

"Can you find your way home from here?"

She nodded yes, adding, "But I don't want to go home by myself."

"You will not be going home by yourself," he promised.

He retrieved his horse and put it with Beth's. They found a comfortable lookout on the rim. From the high point they could see for miles across the bare plain of the desert. They

talked while he occasionally swung his telescope over the alkali, watching for French to ride in from the south.

Beth cried when he told her of Peter's death. "He was
younger than I am and now he is dead."

Skinner did not look at her for he did not want her to see
his own moist eyes. To dispel the sadness, he described
Peter's happy face when he found the gold, and Beth smiled.

Through the telescope he saw a rider coming, the hot, sim-
mering desert air bobbing and weaving the black form of the
horse and man like a spinning top.

"He's coming about three miles out."

"Oh, John, do you have to do it?"

"You know I have to. Here, take Peter's gun and don't hes-
itate one second to use it if it comes to that." He picked up
his rifle and hurried out onto the alkali.

Over many years, several rocks had broken free from the
cap rock and, tumbling down from the height, had rolled out
onto the flat. Some of the more rounded ones lay as much as
a hundred feet from the base of the hill. Skinner carried four
of them, as big as he could lift, another hundred feet or so
farther out and dropped them at random locations.

Behind the largest one and directly between French's line
of approach and the break in the cap rock, he began to dig a
narrow slit trench. It was oriented lengthwise directly behind
the rock. Working swiftly, he scooped out handfuls of the
loose, spongy dirt and threw and scattered it far away so there
would be little sign to betray the presence of the hole.

When it was of satisfactory size, he lay down on his back in
it, his body just barely below the surface of the ground, feet
toward the approaching outlaw. His rifle rested across him,
ready.

The sun was a fireball, burning down and melting him like
lard in a skillet. His clothes were soon soaked with sweat.
From time to time he raised his head, just enough to see over

the rock, and look for French. Finally he could make out the rider with his naked eye.

Beth, from the top of the elevated rim, had watched French approach for several minutes. Her pulse raced as the outlaw drew nearer and nearer to the man lying in the hole in the ground. Fervently she hoped French did not see him.

Skinner, his ear pressed against the ground, could plainly hear the increasing loudness of the hoof beats. He figured he would be spotted the minute he rose to a shooting position. He did not plan a shoot-out with the outlaw; he wanted to kill him as quickly and easily as possible. So he waited.

He judged the rider was close enough. He sat erect, sweeping the rifle up and firing immediately.

French was watching the top of the rim and did not see Skinner's head and shoulders pop above the rock, but the startled horse did and instantly, fast as a striking rattler, shied to the right, flinging French sideways and forward. Skinner's bullet ripped French's shirt and gouged a shallow, hot groove through the flesh of the top of his shoulder.

French, understanding immediately it was an ambush, reacted by reflex, continuing his fall forward. He threw his hand out to catch the mane of the horse and his right foot caught the top of the saddle. The horse bolted away at an angle, the man hanging along its neck and shoulder on the side opposite Skinner.

Skinner twisted right and came to his knees. Damn, he could not let the man escape! He fired at French's leg showing above the saddle. He saw the leg jerk with the shot, but the man continued to cling to the horse as it raced for safety.

With deadly accuracy he slammed another bullet through the soft lower portion of the horse's neck and into French's chest.

The horse stumbled and fell, French tumbling clear. As the
L10 outlaw fought to sit up, John blew his heart apart.

Beth saw John walk to the horse and shoot it, stopping its tortured struggling. He ransacked the man's pockets and then checked the saddlebags. Seemingly satisfied at their contents, he cut them free, tossed them over his arm and walked swiftly toward the path leading up to her.

She hurried to the horses, untied their reins, and turned down the trail to meet him.